THE BIG TIME!

The door opened and Thomas came in . . . He came in backwards, pushing the door open with his back, for his arms were full of things which Sarah couldn't identify. He glanced at her as he struggled across the room to rid himself of the burden . . .

'What's all that?'

'Equipment.'

'Motor stuff?'

'Photographic.'

'You what?'

He dusted at his suit and came to sit on the edge of the bed.

'I didn't want to say anything to you, love, in case I couldn't get it. Only, see, there was this auction poster I spotted the day before yesterday when we was down at Hove, remember? It said there was an old photographer's effects being sold up in lots. Well, when I went off after lunch yesterday, while you had a nap, I went and viewed it. And this it is.'

'You've bought a photographer's!'

Thomas and Sarah: Two for a Spin

MOLLIE HARDWICK

SPHERE BOOKS LIMITED
30/32 Gray's Inn Road, London WC1X 8JL

First published in Great Britain
by Sphere Books Limited 1979

The author wishes to thank Alfred Shaughnessy and London Weekend Television for their co-operation in the writing of this book, and to acknowledge her debt to the following scriptwriters upon whose work she has drawn: Jeremy Paul, Terence Brady and Charlotte Bingham, Angharad Lloyd, Alfred Shaughnessy and Anthony Skene.

TRADE MARK

Filmset in VIP Plantin

Printed in Great Britain by
C. Nicholls & Company Ltd
The Philips Park Press, Manchester

CHAPTER ONE

'You'll never want for anything after the tenth of this month. You're comin' out into blue skies. The crock of gold is yours, dear.'

The prediction of Madame Gladwin, 'Palmiste and Clairvoyante', echoed in the mind of Sarah Moffatt as she luxuriated in the splendid bed in the Hotel Metropole, Brighton. She was sitting propped against all the feather-filled pillows, Thomas Watkins's as well as her own. His part of the bed was vacated now. He had dressed and gone out an hour ago. When he came back, within less than another hour, it would be time for them to leave for good.

The twin trays from which they had eaten their last breakfast there lay on the dressing-table, picked clean down to the last crumb of toast and drain of tea. Sarah sighed, and wondered whether what Madame Gladwin had told her had been anything more than the load of 'hokibens' which she had disdainfully admitted was all she doled out to most clients nowadays: 'Money, good health, and a good love-life. It's what they all wants to hear, dear.'

Money they had for the time being; more of it than at most times since they had left the security of the Bellamy household at 165 Eaton Place, London, to live by their wits off a gullible world. That had been a couple of years ago, and somehow they had staggered along, blundering from one situation into another, punctuated by crises, quarrels, periods of separation, reunions, intense affection and mutual recrimination. For the world had not proved so gullible, after all. It had shown them plainly that it owed them a living no more than it did anyone else. They could perhaps have been much more comfortable and worry-free if they had stayed in those cloistered Belgravia surroundings, employed by an amiable family and companioned by such predictable fellow servants as Mr Hudson, Mrs

Bridges, Rose, Edward, and the dim-witted Ruby. But Thomas Watkins and Sarah Moffatt were two of a kind, feeling themseves superior to these obedient donkeys, fitted for higher stations than those of chauffeur and nursery maid, in fact, too good for servitude in any form.

So they had thrown in their lot together and launched out upon a freelance life, snatching at and exploiting any opportunity which Tom's keen Welsh wits sensed might be used to their advantage. Though she often had occasion to despise him for a sneaky little opportunist, whose big ideas had led to only small gains, usually leaving them back where they had begun, with nothing to show save more experience and disillusionment, Sarah had to admire his shrewdness. Her own character couldn't match it, but she knew she could complement it ideally. With her pretensions to aristocratic blood, from exotic forebears with mystic gifts, and her natural ability to act any part from society lady to music hall artiste, she was the perfect foil to Thomas. He had not quite her effrontery; but he had that ingratiating sort of manner which encouraged strangers' confidence in him, and there was no doubt of his store of knowledge of all manner of skills, mostly technical, enough to make people looking for an expert believe they had found one.

This was how it came about that she was lying here in this splendidly-appointed room in one of England's most famous seaside hotels, celebrated for its patronage by millionaires, the stars of the stage, and that endless host of rich men who wished to impress the partners of their dirty weekends of their habit of doing things in the utmost style.

For once, their brief prosperity had been honestly gained. Thomas's one complete skill, as a motor mechanic and driver, had enabled him to do a rich amateur of motor sport a surpassing favour. A handsome cheque had been the reward, plus the bonus of a week at the Metropole. It had been a week of bliss indeed; of loving and living it up. Their temperaments, equally volatile in different ways, had stayed calm as the summer sea, winking there below their windows. They had eaten and drunk without stinting, had strolled on the front, and played the pier machines, and gone to concerts, and even had a win at the races which had paid them back for nearly as much as they had spent all told. But now, at the stipulated hour of noon, by which the room must be vacated, the holiday must be considered over. Life proper must begin again. All Sarah could hope was that Madame Gladwin had been as lastingly right as she had proved to be up till now.

The door opened and Thomas came in: tall, broad-shouldered, black of hair, brows and moustache, and dark of eyes; a Welsh face, watchful and alert, giving nothing away that he didn't want known.

He came in backwards, pushing the door open with his back, for his arms were full of things which Sarah couldn't identify. He glanced at her as he struggled across the room to rid himself of the burden.

'Who's pig in the straw, then?' he mocked.

'I wouldn't mind lying in this straw for good, and that's the truth,' Sarah yawned, stretching her arms above her head. 'I'm enjoying every last blessed minute of it. What's all that?'

'Equipment.'

'Motor stuff?'

'Photographic.'

'You what?'

He dusted his suit and came to sit on the edge of the bed.

'I didn't want to say anything to you, love, in case I couldn't get it. Only, see, there was this auction poster I spotted the day before yesterday when we was down at Hove, remember? It said there was an old photographer's effects being sold up in lots. Well, when I went off after lunch yesterday, while you had a nap, I went and viewed it. And this is it.'

'You've bought a photographer's!'

'No. Just enough gear to set up. Absolute give-away. Half-plate Instantograph camera, good as new: brass-bound, double-swing, folding tailboard, see-saw shutter.

Five quid they cost new, as much as I paid for the whole bloomin' lot – lenses, tripod, ten dozen plates, magnesium flash lamp . . .'

Sarah was more intrigued than astonished. For a moment, sudden hope flourished.

'What you mean to do, Tom? Set up as a beach photographer? You mean we can stay down here?'

But he was shaking his head. 'Nothing cheap as that. Studio work. Fashion, society, *Strand Magazine*, *Sporting and Dramatic* . . .'

'*You?*'

'Of course me. Don't think I bought 'em for you?'

'But you're not a photographer.'

'How do you know I'm not? You don't know half about me yet, girl.'

'I know you've got a head twice the size of a melon, and just as soft inside. I 'spect you think you can teach yourself, just like that.'

'Don't need to learn, I *know*. Dab hand with a camera, Thomas Watkins. Used to have a lovely little quarter-plates Stores Special. Had to get rid of it when things wasn't good before I went to Bellamy's. Still, this is a far better job. Professional. I'd show it you, only it's time you was crawling out of your sty and getting ready. If we're not out by twelve they charge an extra day.'

He took her hand and gave a little pull. Sarah sighed again, patted the bedclothes over her thighs, and swung her legs out.

'Well, it was good while it lasted, I'll say that. Wonder when the next time'll be?'

Thomas grinned secretly. 'You never know. Fashionable photographer, moving in swishy circles.'

'Yeh, and leaving their girl, who ain't even their bloomin' wife, while you go off hobnobbing with society tarts. I haven't forgotten you and that Felicity Pomeroy at that Ashdown Forest place.'

'No more than you and your Lord Bloody Purley, going off in our car leaving me stranded.'

'Tit for tat.' She pulled her nightdress over her head and stood unabashedly naked. They had often talked of marriage – argued over it, rather – but it had never come to pass. Each was too independent. They wanted to keep their options open and their freedom intact. It might be valuable, in case of let-down by the other. 'And there's no need to look at me like that,' she went on, flaunting herself. 'You've had more'n your fill of that this week.'

'I wasn't,' he grinned. 'Merely thinking how you'd do for a model. I reckon you might pass.'

Sarah had turned away to gather up her underclothes. She twisted her head sharply back, though.

'What do you mean, model? Here, just what sort of pictures are you reckoning on taking?'

'Not *that* sort.'

'I should bloomin' hope not – of me or anybody else.'

'What I've got to do,' he told her seriously while she dressed, 'is make a bit of a splash quickly. Get my name known. You can't just gate-crash the Savoy and start clicking away.'

'I wouldn't put that past you, either.'

'No, you got to get noticed. Get something special into a paper. A scoop. Or win a big competition.'

'And what do we do in the meantime? We can't have enough left to live for ever, even after that win on the nags.'

'We've got enough for a month or two. I'll just have to make it in that time, eh?'

'You sure you can take photos – real ones?'

'You'll see. I promise.'

'I'll never get your limits, Tom Watkins. Hey, where we goin' to live? Stay down here? It'd be nice.'

But he was shaking his head. 'Got to be back in the Smoke. Near Fleet Street. Never know when a chance might crop up.'

Sarah shook her head resignedly. 'Well, where then? We got nowhere there any more.'

'We'll find somewhere to rent. Somewhere cheap, so's to keep the overheads down.'

She surveyed the grand surroundings gloomily.

'After this! I said it was like a dream. Back to bloody Kilburn, I 'spect. Cobbles and filth and rain.'

'I thought we might try south of the river. More life going on. Never know when some rich human drama might unfold before my very lens, and we're made overnight.'

'Yeh. All the rich human drama I can see is us starvin'.' She gestured towards the equipment. 'I bet you that lot's in hock in six weeks, and you and me, too.'

'When have I ever let you down?' he grinned, and didn't wait for the certain answer. 'Will you hurry up? We'll get a bite, then back to Town to look at the rent ads in the evenings.'

CHAPTER TWO

It was an irony, in the light of Sarah's pessimistic forecast, that the London lodging place they found was actually over a pawnshop.

'Told you!' she claimed almost triumphantly. 'At least we shan't have far to go whenever we need to hock the lot.'

'Got no imagination, you haven't,' Tom grinned back. 'Keep well in with the old chap and he'll lend me bits of props for pictures. Them and the costumes we've still got from Barnaby's are all I'll need.'

Barnaby's was the music hall in Kilburn where Thomas had re-discovered Sarah, dancing in the chorus. True to form, they had ensured that when she left a few nice costumes had been smuggled out as well, in the basket containing the equipment for the 'Cabinet of Mystery', an illusion act which they had bought. The sensational success they had expected to enjoy with it at Chatham Music Hall, in Kent, had proved illusory, in a different sense. The equipment had been long since sold off, but most of the costumes still remained.

So did the basket. But for its presence, their little apartment would have been bare indeed: a narrow iron bed, a table, a couple of chairs, a curtained-off rail for a wardrobe, a scratched and glass-ringed chest of drawers, an iron stove for heating and cooking; there was very little more. Sarah's spirits plummeted when she first surveyed it, only hours after quitting the Metropole, all gilt and finery and grace and 'With pleasure madam'.

'Tom . . .' she began to protest, but he was drawing aside a curtain and chortling with delight.

'A bath, Sarah. Our own bath.'

'Well, that's something,' she conceded. There was

nothing much else to feel pleased about, except that they had a roof over their heads and that Peckham, an area of much new building of bright little villas, going for £200 a time, was less depressing than Kilburn. Although, of course, it wasn't in one of the villas that they had had to land themselves. Oh, no; it was in an old area due for clearance. The three brass balls signifying their landlord's trade above his grimy window hadn't shone for years.

'It's more than something,' Tom was answering, trying the taps. Rusty brown water spluttered out of each, and though it cleared after some moments it was cold in both cases. 'It's what I need – my darkroom. Squeeze a little table in to hold the d. & p. things . . .'

'The what and what?'

'Developing and printing. Got nearly everything I need already. Just a few bob to spend on chemicals.'

'You're not going to be mixing bloomin' stinkin' chemicals in here! This is where we got to sleep and eat, Gawd help us.'

'There won't be any smell. Well, hardly. You can buy all the solutions ready made up nowadays.'

'Can't you take your pictures out for someone else to do for you?' she pleaded.

He looked affronted. 'No photographic artist ever lets anyone do his d. & p. for him. It's half the art. It isn't just setting something up in front of the lens and squeezing the bulb, you know. Yes, another length of curtain round the side and top to make it real dark. A clothes line across and a few pegs for drying . . .'

Sarah wandered away, leaving him muttering. She unpacked their few personal belongings. Distributed between the wardrobe and chest of drawers they still left space to spare. As veritable rolling stones, they had gathered little moss to cart with them. She selected the prettiest of the dresses from the skip and hung them up, too. If he was serious about her doing some modelling for him, they could come in handy.

He himself was bustling about, unpacking his photographic things, setting up his dark room, bursting to get started. The prized camera was revealed now, placed on its wooden tripod in the centre of the uncarpeted floor. Sarah had to admit that it was a handsome piece of equipment, of brass, stained wood and leather. When Tom let her turn the focusing wheel she was impressed by its smooth response and the way it extended and contracted the bellows.

Tom's dark eyes were shining. She impulsively went over and gave him a hug. For all that he could be a swine at times, and moody and bitter towards her, she genuinely admired his resource and that recurring optimism which brought back hope to her when she felt down about everything. She sensed, too, that often when he turned and savaged her he was taking out on her what he felt against himself. He hated failure, especially when it was due to his own fault. It humiliated him to have her there to witness it, and to make her feel that he had let her down.

She felt his impatience to get on with what he was doing, but she held him and gave him a kiss.

'You deserve to succeed, Tom,' she told him. 'There's thousands do who haven't half your spark.'

'Ta, love,' he responded, and returned the kiss. 'Don't you worry. We'll make it yet.'

'Back to the dear old Metropole some day, eh?'

'You bet.'

He released himself and went back to his task.

Four weeks after this, not only were they not back at the dear old Metropole, but some of the items from their little store had been transferred downstairs into the other establishment owned by Mr Irvine. Whenever Sarah went out she averted her eyes from the mud-bespattered window, for fear he might have advanced something else of hers or Tom's to the forefront of his pitiful display.

Their money had gone faster than expected. Thomas, to do him credit, had slogged away at his photography. He had begun with Sarah – an unspoken compliment, she supposed – posing her this way and that, in each one of her costumes.

Each time he had hurried into his makeshift darkroom, only to emerge slowly, after sounds of running taps and gently splashing fluids, to say that he hadn't 'got her' yet in the way he had in mind. When she asked to see what he had got, he said he had torn it up. He wouldn't let her look until it was right. What artist would?

He had ventured afield: to Clapham Common, where nursemaids pushing prams had glared at him when he gesticulated to them to pause for a picture; to Brixton and Camberwell, where men with clay pipes in their mouths and thumbs stuck into their waistcoats sauntered up and asked him 'oo the 'ell 'e thought 'e was, a-pointin' of that thing at their missuses and gals? He had crossed the river one Sunday into Trafalgar Square, when some inflamed political rally had been taking place, only to be moved on by a policeman who had warned him, friendly enough, that his camera's presence might spark off violence.

By one, by two, their little possessions had been taken down to Mr Irvine, middle-aged, Scottish and more patient with his lodgers than with his clients. As Thomas had hoped, he had proved willing to lend odd items in pawn for an hour or two's photographic session. He drew the line, though, at lending back any of their own things pledged to him for the few bob they brought.

'Fair's fair, mon. If I gi' ye it back, ye mecht as weel ne'er hae takken ma guid cash for it at a'.'

This cold, wet morning, though, in the late winter of 1911, Tom had prevailed with him just once more. For the umpteenth time Sarah lay forward, her arms resting on the table which, draped with the white tulle swathes of one of the remaining theatrical costumes, might have been the most elegant of chaise longues. A bundled-up newspaper, hidden beneath the material, counterfeited for a cushion. Her right arm was extended languorously, touched at the crook of its elbow joint by the fingers of her left hand, the third finger of which sported (courtesy of Mr Irvine) four rings. The right hand held a stiff posy of much-photographed imitation blooms.

Her cheek lay on her shoulder, her face towards the camera. Her dark brown hair was tied with a single ribbon, the blue eyes dreamy and the lips inviting with a coquettish smile. A single strand of greasy imitation pearls broke the line of her neck and shoulders. It was an attitude no woman would have assumed naturally for one minute, or been able to sustain unnaturally for ten; but it was 'artistic', and Thomas was working feverishly to make the most of the light through their window, which too soon must fade.

'Now,' he ordered hurriedly, 'move the roses a bit further forward. No, towards the camera, I mean. That's it. Turn your eyes a touch more upward . . . tilt your chin . . . Wait there . . .'

He ducked back under the black velvet drape behind the camera, only to re-emerge moments later shaking his head.

'No, it's not right yet. Try and look more natural, like.'

'In this position? I never felt less natural in me life.' She uncoiled herself and struggled up, petite and graceful in the tulle, revealing the crumpled heap of newspaper on the table top. She threw the faded flowers on to it. 'It's a load of tosh, Tom. You got to admit it.'

'No, it isn't. Come on – before the light goes.'

'Before the soup boils dry. You might have thought to give it a stir.'

She went over to the stove top, where a blackened pan exuded steam. With the hand which bore the four rings she grasped the worn wooden spoon and stirred a thick brew of peas.

'Just one more go,' he begged.

'No. Dinner's more important. Look, I'm not fooled that I look like a society tart, and the judges of the competition won't be, neither. It's all arty gubbins.'

'It's not, love. It's what wins prizes – poetic vision of truth.'

'Then come and take a picture of this bleedin' soup. That's our truth. All we got for dinner, thanks to your precious Edith.'

'Edith?'

'Your new mistress. Oh, don't gawp like that. I mean your camera there. She's the one you've been in love with these past weeks.'

At once, though, his dismayed expression moved her. She put down the soup spoon and went to touch him.

'Sorry, love. I don't begrudge you her. Only she's got to deliver the goods soon, or we'll be stony bust again. I know it's hard for you to face, Tom. You get the worst of it – dirty looks, doors slammed in your face and all that. But dressing me up isn't the answer. You got to find a new approach.'

The sympathy was wasted. The light had gone already, and he knew he could achieve no romantic effect by magnesium flash.

'I was doing fine till you moved. Just another minute'd have got it. I might not have won the perishing competition, but it could have been good enough for runner-up. Even that'd have got my name in print.'

'If you want my opinion,' Sarah answered mildly, 'the *Daily Mail* readers are bored stiff seeing the same real nobs and duchesses, without me trying to fake 'em. You want something . . . sensational. I know – me drownding in the bath – *if* you can spare it from your chemicals, that is.'

She lifted the pan and poured the soup into their only two bowls. Thomas sat down resignedly at the table which had so recently been the platform for his artistic conception, sweeping off the newspaper to accommodate his soup bowl. Sarah sat opposite him. The brew was scalding and substantial.

'It's all we got,' she pointed out. 'Get it down you hot. You been coughing a lot lately.'

'It's quite good,' he conceded, head down. Sarah was right: he had been coughing. It wasn't like Tom to take cold, though her own bones felt it enough in this place at this cheerless time of year.

'Look,' she resumed, anxious to rally him, 'what's this competition called?'

' "My Most Unforgettable Face".'

'Hm! Sounds like me, all right. Seriously, though, don't you think, if we went out after we've finished this, we might find some really unforgettable mug?'

'Where?'

'Downstairs, for a start. Irvine's customers. I seen plenty of 'em there already. Poor bleeders, you wouldn't forget some of them after all your duchesses and countesses had gone home.'

'I tell you, it's glamour they want, not realism. It's what's fashionable.'

'That's what I'm trying to get into you. All the others'll go for what's fashionable, and they'll all take the same picture, near as dammit. You do something really different. They'll give you one of the prizes just for being original. Paper like the *Mail*, they know their business. I mean, it's human nature to want to see someone worse off than you are. 'Stead of saying, "Coo, ain't she loverely" they'll say "Just look at the pore old soul! Might be me, if I let meself go. Good ole *Daily Mail*, givin' timely warnin'!" '

'You may be right,' Thomas had to admit. What Sarah lacked in devious vision such as his, she made up for in human instinct. 'I suppose we could find some toothless old biddy who'd pose for a tanner.'

'I know one who'd do the part for nothing,' she grinned back. 'Only she's not an old biddy, and she's proud of her own teeth.' She flashed them at him. 'Save waiting around to find someone and having to talk 'em into it. You got to get your entry in by tomorrow, remember? Take the picture first thing, and you can deliver it in the afternoon.'

And so, in the clear light of next morning, before the air had had time to cloud with dust, smoke and fumes, Tom erected his tripod on the pavement outside the pawn shop while Sarah, hair towsled under a battered hat, face skilfully grimed from the stove top, wearing a filthy apron over her most sagging dress, practised poses: walking from the shop, handkerchief to her eyes; looking wistfully into the window at a pair of boots; staring up at the brass balls as if supplicating her Maker to ordain that she would be offered an extra twopence for the unidentifiable bundle contained in the basket on her arm.

It was cold, out there, the sort of cold that bites into the bones, but Tom prepared slowly, the perfectionist, unheeding that he had stepped back into a puddle, his worn boots soaking it up. He coughed frequently, but didn't seem to notice, absorbed in what he was doing.

'Come on,' Sarah pleaded. 'It's perishin'. Oh, look, it's started bleedin' rainin'.'

'All the better. Give it a few minutes to wet the window. Look even more pathetic.' He was positively wheezing now.

'You'll be pathetic if it ruins your camera – and I don't like that cough.'

'I'm all right, and the camera'll dry off. Now, gaze at the boots as if . . . as if they was your late husband's, all you'd had left of him, and now you've just had to pop even them. "The Poor Young Widow of Peckham", I'll call it.'

She nearly responded that, from the sound of him, she soon would be in that situation in real life. Since he wasn't her husband, however, the riposte would be pointless. She just obeyed. He dived back under the velvet hood.

'Just like that!' came his muffled command. 'Got it.' He came out again. 'One more for luck. Don't move while I change the plate.'

The rain was really splashing down by now. He fumbled what he was doing, and paused briefly to rub his chest hard, as if trying to dislodge something inside. Then he went back under the cloth. She sensed his fingers squeeze the rubber bulb, and heard the incisive click of the shutter against the background rattle of the street.

'Right,' he gasped, emerging. 'Let's get in.'

Bundling up his equipment, which seemed too heavy for him now, he staggered after her up to the dry and relative comfort of their cheerless apartment. When Thomas had deposited his burden he sat on one of the chairs and wheezed and wheezed. But when Sarah, whose teeth were chattering, went and put her hand on his brow, and found it burning, he shook her away and roused himself to enter his darkroom and set about recreating on paper the image he hoped he had managed to imprison on the coated glass plate.

He was a long time about it. Sarah stoked up the inadequate stove as much as she dared without squandering their dwindling fuel supply, and sat over it, hugging her shoulders. The watery sounds from the darkroom, and the spatter of rain on the window, served to intensity her coldness. She felt pains in her own chest in sympathy with Tom's coughs and wheezes. At long last, though, she heard a satisfied exclamation. He burst out, waving a sheet of photographic paper by its top corners, between fingers and thumbs.

'Here it is! Look – a blooming masterpiece!'

She stared at her reflection in the paper mirror: the great soulful eyes in the bereaved countenance, the lines she had so carefully painted, the smudged cheeks, the straggling hair. It was so expressive that it caused her to shiver anew.

'Cor! That's what I could get to look like.'

'You said they'll say that. Hope they do.'

'Ugh! It's frightening, though.'

'The photographer's art,' he reminded her. But though he smiled proudly, there was a wan look about him.

'You're going to bed, Tom Watkins,' Sarah ordered. 'You're sickening, for a fact.'

'I don't feel my best, that's sure. But I've got to deliver this first.'

'I'll take it for you.'

'No, I'll deliver it in person. Only worry if I don't see it in their hands in time. Ouch, my chest's tight.'

Sarah scrambled for their outdoor things.

'All right, then. But I'm coming with you – just in case.'

It was as well that she did. No one would have been able to let her know when he collapsed in Fleet Street and was taken unconscious to a hospital in Aldgate, run by a religious order, where he was immediately pronounced to have pneumonia and be in danger for his life. But Sarah was there to support him as he crumpled down on the bottom step of the *Daily Mail* building; and they had just successfully delivered the photograph.

CHAPTER THREE

In typically mercurial fashion, the *Daily Mail*'s proprietor and founder, Lord Northcliffe, had had the idea for the photographic competition, telephoned orders that it was to be launched, and then had completely forgotten about it under the pressure of political matters connected with his ownership of that loftier organ, *The Times*. The Arts Editor of the *Mail* groaned at the prospect of an avalanche of deplorable snapshots piling into his office and hastily passed responsibility for the contest to one of his underlings. This was a man named Warboys: fiftyish, liverish, long ago disabused of any notion that Fleet Street was a street of adventure and glamour. Thank God, though, it had plenty of pubs.

He came in at his usual hour of eleven in the morning, with the usual acid stomach and sour temper from his long omnibus journey from Essex. What he saw in his small office stopped him on the threshold.

'What in Gawd's name's this lot?' he demanded. Violet, his young and yet unjaded secretary smiled. One thing she had learned already was that it didn't do to let him browbeat her.

'The competition. The final entry.'

She had had the clever initiative to prevent the stuff flooding in on him day by day. It would only have meant for continuing irascibility. Better to let it accumulate in the mail room, to be delivered in several sacks at one go. 'It closed last night, you remember.'

'Oh Gawd! I thought if I didn't think about it, it'd forget itself and go away. Better still, that no one would enter the damn' fool thing.'

'Well, you see, they have. Hundreds, I'm afraid.'

'I can't waste my time on all that.' He got out his turnip watch and consulted it. 'Got an appointment.'

Violet had also learned that that referred to any of three favourite pubs. But she reminded him boldly, 'When we announced it, we did say it would be judged promptly after closing date.'

'So it will, but not by me.'

'By whom, sir?'

He gave her a sharp look. He sometimes suspected she was taking a rise out of him for his imprecise grammar. Right – he would get his own back.

'By yourn.'

'Me!'

Warboys leered. 'That's right. Want to get on in journalism, Gawd help you. Here's a chance to start, then. Doin' you a favour.'

She looked apprehensively at the sacks.

'Nothing urgent?' he asked. 'Right then. I'll be off to my meeting. Sort out the likeliest half dozen and put 'em on my desk. I'll choose the best three. Right?' He winked maliciously and went out.

Violet went to one of the sacks and untied it. It was full of photographic prints, each with a label attached giving the entrant's particulars. She scooped out a handful and glanced quickly through them. Even to her untrained eye they were awful: blurred babies staring sightlessly from prams, self-conscious housewives trying to look mysterious, even a grinning dog. But one picture did catch and hold her attention. It was of a poor young woman, prematurely lined from deprivation and sorrow, gazing hopelessly at a pair of boots in a rain-spattered shop window.

She looked at the label: 'The Poor Young Widow of Peckam – T. Watkins', and an address. Violet reached across to place it on Mr Warboys's desk. She returned to the task with enthusiasm growing. If there were a dozen or two as good as that mongst the dross, the contest would have been worthwhile.

Even as his work was being thus singled out, Thomas lay in coma-like sleep in the medical ward. One of the nurses, a nun, paused in her progress along the beds to bend over him and listen to his painful breathing. Pneumonia had been unhesitatingly diagnosed. She shook her head, and passed on.

In the apartment over the pawnshop Sarah played out a scenario of imagination.

'Oh, thank you. How very kind of you. Yes, two weeks ago, of pneumonia. Oh, he was a truly wonderful husband. So talented. Such a loss. Yes, photographer latterly, but he'd done so many other things in his time, you know: racing motorist, airman, explorer . . .'

A knocking at the door interrupted her. 'Come in!' she called. Mr Irvine entered. Sarah remembered with a start that it was rent day. He always came promptly at this hour.

'Oh, Mr Irvine,' she said, easily forcing tears to her eyes, 'I was tryin' to get up strength to come down and tell you. My husband . . . in hospital. Double pneumonia . . . and complications.'

Irvine frowned suspiciously.

'He was a' recht this morning, takking yer picture ootside ma shop.'

'I know. It come on so sudden. He collapsed on the steps of the *Daily Mail* – he does a lot of work for them, you know.'

'Does he, now? Weel, I'm verra sorry, Mrs Watkins. I'm no' a hard man, especially where the ladies are concerned, but business is business, ye ken.'

'Oh, the rent! I'd quite forgotten. I'm afraid, you see, he didn't leave any cash behind with me. If you can just manage to wait till he comes home . . .'

'*Double* pneumonia, d'ye say?' His expression clearly stated that he did not expect to see Thomas again, let alone his money. 'As I say, I'm sorry, Mrs Watkins, but ye're in hock tae the eyeballs already.'

Sarah lowered her head and nodded humbly. 'I know, I know. You have practically everything we possess, except his photographic equipment, which is essential to his profession.'

He glanced assessingly at the camera on its tripod. 'I'll lend ye a couple o' weeks' rent on it.'

'I couldn't. He'd never forgive me parting with it.'

'It's more than generous. Till he gets on his feet. It's no use tae you, is it?'

'But it's worth so much more. I mean, the camera alone cost fifty pound.'

Mr Irvine knew something of the value of cameras, through his trade. 'Tak' it or leave it,' he responded implacably.

Sarah made a show of inward struggle, then supplicated, 'Two weeks, then . . . and a few of my personal things back. Go on, Mr Irvine. I may have to make a new life for myself. You wouldn't see me destitute, would you?'

He allowed himself to relent. The trinkets of hers he had down in the shop were worth almost nothing anyway.

'A' recht, then. Done. The missus always says I'm too kind for this profession.'

'It's good-hearted people like you makes the world go round,' Sarah assured him profoundly.

'What's this, then?' Mr Warboys demanded, staring down at the single photograph on his blotting pad.

'The winner,' Violet said. 'You told me to choose.'

'The best half-dozen, I said.'

'There's no need. There isn't one to compare with this.'

'Taking a lot on yourself, young lady. Mm. Soppy, but not bad.'

'I think it's very moving.'

'Ugh. In that case, I expect our lady readers will. All right. That's it, then.'

The news reached Sarah at the very moment next day shen she was redeeming her few bits of costume jewellery. Thomas's camera was already in the forefront of the window, besi 'e the very boots which had featured in its last composition. She stared at the telegram, just brought to her at the counter. Mr Irvine watched her, fully expecting it to be the fateful message from the hospital. She managed to conceal her excitement, informing him offhandedly, 'Just the Editor. The *Daily Mail*, you know. Thomas allowed one of his pictures to go into a contest they're running, and it's won, of course. Twenty-five pounds.'

Irvine looked hard at her, suspicious that this might be some ploy to gain his confidence and some more of his credit. But she held out the form for him to see, with its signature: 'Editor, *Daily Mail*.'

'I'll go and collect it, then get straight down to the infirmary,' she said. 'I'll just take these few things for now and get the camera later. It'll do you a favour back, being able to have it in your window for a while. Raise the tone of your shop.'

She skipped away.

'Mrs Watkins?' Warboys repeated.

'That's right. The wife of the one who took the picture. I've come to collect the prize.'

'Where's your husband, then?'

'In the infirmary. Very seriously ill.'

Warboys glanced at Violet for moral support. She was looking at their visitor intently.

'I'm sorry to hear it,' he conceded. 'Only, problem is . . . I mean, how do we know you're who you say you are? Can't hand out money to anybody just like that.'

'She's the Poor Young Widow of Peckham,' Violet told him simply. 'Aren't you?'

Sarah had to admit it. If she hadn't been impatient they'd have sent the money through the post, and never found out.

'Fake, then, was it?' Warboys accused. That too-clever girl of his had nearly landed him in it.

'Well, if you put it that way, yes,' Sarah agreed. 'But that's where the skill comes in, doesn't it? I mean, all photography's faked a bit. It's a . . . a poetic vision of the truth. That's how I see it, anyway.'

'You know about photography, Mrs Watkins?'

'Naturally, living with my husband.'

'He's, ah, not a professional, by any chance?'

'Only one of the best in the business.'

'Then he's disqualified. The competition rules were quite clear: open to amateurs only.'

'Ah, yes. but I didn't mean he makes a *livin'* out of it. I was referrin' to his skill as bein' on a *par* with professionals. You must have seen that for yourself, givin' him the prize. In fact, if I was you, I'd snap him up double quick for your paper while you still got the chance. I know he's considerin' offers from several others.'

Sarah flicked a glance towards Violet, whom she sensed to be on her side, but was not too pleased to note her amused look.

'Shall I give Mrs Watkins the money?' Violet asked her chief, who shrugged.

'I suppose you'll have to.'

Sarah erupted. 'Just a minute, Mr What'syourname. This is a national contest my hubby's won. I didn't expect caviar and bubbly when I came here, but at least a civil word and a handshake. You've accused us of cheatin'. Well, let me tell you that picture may have been a fake when it was took, but it's looked bloomin' close to comin' true these past two days. It's a real human story what happened. So just give me the money, and I won't take up any more of your valuable time.'

When genuinely ferocious, she was formidable. Warboys nodded hasty assent to Violet, who was already counting out twenty-five pound notes from a cash box. She handed it to Sarah with a sympathetic smile.

'Well deserved. I wish your husband a speedy recovery.'

Sarah glowered still, but suddenly relaxed and smiled back.

'Ta, love.'

'She'll have to sign a receipt,' Mr Warboys declared acidly. They both smiled at him, pityingly.

Thomas didn't recognise her when she went to see him soon afterwards, let alone recognise the copy of his winning photograph. She was told he was probably nearing the crisis-point of his illness, and that there was nothing she could do but pray. She went back to their rooms, but did not pray. She meant to, but found herself too detached to get up the necessary fervour. If he survived, they would struggle on. If he snuffed it, she would manage alone. Since they alternated between being a help and a handicap to one another, the balance of independence and interdependence was equal, only needing the emotion of the moment to tip it either way.

When she went back to the hospital next afternoon, though, and was told that he had survived the crisis, she felt true relief. She did want him, after all.

He looked uncharacteristically vulnerable in the bed of white-painted iron. His skin was an indescribable colour and he looked at her blankly, with hooded eyes.

'Don't look too chipper, do he?' came a man's voice from behind her chair. Sarah turned to see the man in the adjoining bed watching her with unnaturally bright eyes. He was grizzle-haired, sixty-odd, she guessed. The hand he lifted for her to shake was more bone than flesh.

'Arthur Dooley, missus. Pleased to meet you.'

But as she shook his hand she heard a whisper behind, and turned back to Thomas.

'Sarah . . .?'

'Hello, love. It's me, all right.'

'I saw . . . the gates of heaven last night. Angels . . .'

'Them's not angels. They're nuns. Listen, Tom. Try to understand. I got news'll make you better. We won the prize.'

'Prize?'

'*Daily Mail.* Most Unforgettable Face. Look, I brought some copies of the paper.'

She brought one from her carrier bag and gave it to him. On second thought, she got out another and gave it to Mr Dooley.

'Clever, isn't he, my Tom? Took that, and I posed for it. See what it says: 'Our competition designed to explore the wonders of the human visage has brought forward an overwhelming response. The winning photograph, reproduced here, was chosen with difficulty from amongst hundreds which had survived elimination: a picture to tug at the very heart-strings . . .'

'He took that?'

'Yeh.'

'And that's you?'

'Wouldn't think it – I hope not.'

'I certainly wouldn't.' This was another voice, female, and amused. Sarah lifted her head to see a young nurse with a nun's grey wimple; a pink, scrubbed face and grey eyes. 'Is that really you, Mrs Watkins?'

'It definitely is, Sister . . .'

'Nurse Cecilia. May I congratulate you, then? That picture will move a few hearts which need moving.'

'Well, ta. But it's my Thomas who ought to be thanked. He set it up and took it. Nurse, how is he?'

'He's quite all right, now. He'll have to take things quietly for a time, of course. I'm sorry to say, Mrs Watkins, we'll have to ask you to take over care of him very soon, at home. We need the beds here so very desperately, you know.'

'Oh, I'll look after the old s— my Tom. Just glad to see him back in the land of the livin'.'

A faint voice interrupted: Tom's. 'Thank Nurse Cecilia, Sar. Her unforgettable face has contributed in no small measure to my recovery.'

'Blimey!' Sarah exclaimed. 'He is recovering quick.'

'I'll miss him,' came Mr Dooley's voice from behind her. 'Hasn't had much to say for himself, mind, but he's been a good listener. Cor, fancy him taking this!'

He gesticulated with the newspaper. The nurse moved on her placid way. Thomas's eyes had closed again. Mr Dooley told Sarah, 'He'll sleep in fits and starts, you'll find. They're always the same. I seen plenty of 'em pass through, though not all so lucky.'

'What's your trouble, then, Mr . . .?'

'Dooley. Ticker. Thought I was getting out soon, only

they say I got to stay. Pity, when they need the beds so bad, but what can a man do?'

'Your wife can't nurse you at home, then?'

'No wife, no home. Don't look sorry, missus, it's not so bad as it sounds. Foot-loose and fancy-free's always been my motto. Stay a bachelor and don't hang women and property round your neck. More fun that way – and it has been.'

'I dare say; till it comes to needing someone to look after you.'

'I never looked after no one, and I don't expect it back; 'cept for these good ladies here. I reckon they do it for the good of their souls, so that's their reward taken care of.'

He paused and looked from Sarah to the sleeping Thomas, then back again, before continuing.

'All the same, don't suppose you'd be interested in helping me, would you?'

'We ain't got room,' Sarah replied quickly. 'Honest. Just one room over a pawnshop . . .'

'I don't mean that. I'm not hinting. What I mean is, I got some things to arrange. Dispose of. Shan't be needing 'em any more. But I want somebody I could trust. I'd make it worth your while.'

Sarah hesitated. The nurse was coming back, carrying equipment and with that purposeful look which indicated that visiting time was over and it was back to serious business.

'Tell you what,' she said. 'Talk to Tom about it when he's a bit more himself. They won't chuck him out in this state, will they?'

'Not for a day or two, I reckon. All right, I will. Anyway, get him to give me a visit, will you, missus? There's no one else, and I never knew anyone famous in me life before.'

The old man's choice of adjective didn't seem out of place, if the response of the *Daily Mail*'s readers to Thomas's study of the Poor Young Widow of Peckham was any yardstick for fame. Letters poured in, and were carried by messenger boys to the counter of Mr Irvine, who took them in with growing incredulity and conveyed them almost deferentially upstairs. Sarah had them sorted and waiting for Thomas when he was brought home two days later. She put him straight to bed and got in beside him with the pile of letters on their knees.

'Look at this,' she said proudly. 'Labour politician wants me to go on his platform at his bye-election to shame the government.'

'Curate here, at Grantham, says he wants to marry you,' Thomas said, his voice still weak.

'Yeh. And this crackpot reckons I'm his wife already, from another life.'

'Any of 'em sent the Poor Young Widow any money, would be more to the point?'

'Only offers of situations. Still, it'll all stand you in good stead, Tom. One of the newspapers'll be certain to take you on now, won't they? Maybe the *Mail*, even.'

She left the bed and tucked him in. 'But first, you got to get your strength back. I've spent some of the prize money – no, you might as well know – on meat broth and things. I even got some stout, 'cos they say it builds you up quick. So just you have a nice sleep now, and then . . .'

But the instruction was superfluous. He had dropped off already. Sarah went quietly to the prop basket for some things, then slipped out of the door, on her way to look into one of those well-wishers' offers which she had decided not to mention to him.

CHAPTER FOUR

'So you are the Poor Young Widow of Peckham.'

Sarah nodded forlornly. The clothes she had put on to come to this suburban house were those she had worn for the photograph. Before putting on the hat she had rumpled her hair and had run a finger along the stove-top, collecting some blacking to smudge on to one cheek. All the way to Denmark Hill she had kept hoping that someone would recognise her from her picture and stop her for a sympathetic chat; but no one had.

A maid had shown her into the tall Victorian house and into a parlour, where a powerfully built lady of about forty introduced herself as the Mrs Green who had written the letter which had brought her there. A friendly man came in, smoking a pipe, who proved to be her husband.

'Heavens, my dear, you look every bit as in need as your picture indicated. We were most touched by it, weren't we, Hector?'

'Yes, dear.'

'I said at once that we must do something to help.'

'Very kind, mum, I'm sure.'

'Not at all. We considered sending some money, but my husband reminded me that there is such a thing as pride, even in adversity. Didn't you, Hector?'

The man nodded and smiled at Sarah. His wife went on, 'So it seemed to us a better plan to offer you some work, so that you could have the satisfaction of knowing you had earned the money honestly.'

'Quite right, mum. That's how I'd soonest it was.'

'I'm afraid we can only promise one week. Our maid, Grace, has no assistance at the moment. A girl is due to come in a week's time. So if you would like to oblige in the meanwhile, you are most welcome. You would find us not ungenerous in the matter of a wage. Wouldn't she, dear?'

'Yes, dear.'

'It's most kind,' Sarah said. 'But I couldn't live in, though.'

'Oh?'

'No. You see, my husb . . . my late husband's brother – my brother-in-law, that is – he's very seriously ill. Just discharged from infirmary with double pneumonia, and nowhere to go, so I took him in myself in my little room, and I'm nursing him. What else could I have done?'

'Oh, you poor thing! On top of all your other difficulties.'

Sarah emitted a deep sigh. 'Life 'as to go on, as they say. If we don't stretch a 'elpin' 'and to one another in trouble, then we can't expect no 'ands put out for us when our time comes.'

'How true, how very true.'

'I don't know as I ought to leave 'im there on 'is own at all, but I got to get a bit of money from somewhere, and when your kind letter came it sounded too good to be true.'

'I'm so glad we can help a little. As to your not being able to live in, we shall have to accept that that just cannot be helped. Shan't we, Hector?'

'Yes, dear.'

'So if you can arrange to come here each morning by eight – well, let us say half-past, since you have to travel from Peckham – and will work through until six, then that will do. You will get a substantial midday meal, too.'

'Thank you ever so, mum. Sir.'

'Quite all right. So you'll begin tomorrow?'

'On the dot, mum.'

'Good. Now, I think I had better tell Grace to find you something a little . . . better to wear while you are here. And while she is doing so, I'm sure you would be glad of the opportunity of a nice hot bath.'

'Ooh yes, mum.'

'Hector, ring for Grace, will you? We'll soon have you feeling like a new woman, my dear.'

Sarah was glad of the offer of a bath. She had been to a

public baths a week earlier, but had had nothing but cold washes since. The bath in the lodging would have been useless to her, even with the photographic stuff cleared out of it.

Her impersonation of the Poor Young Widow was not a nefarious deception of these sympathetic folk. She had spent more of the prize money than she had hinted to Thomas. Mr Irvine had seized the opportunity to demand the rent arrears, and had offered her a small reduction if she chose to pay a couple of weeks' more in advance. She had accepted; and that, together with redeeming some of the pawned items, had left her with less than fifteen of the twenty-five pounds. Tom would be furious when he found out, even though it wasn't as if she'd squandered the money. This little job had been offered to her, so she had resolved to take it, despite the number of times she had said she would sooner starve than go back into service. Mr and Mrs Green had promised to be generous, and she might be able to get the savings up a bit by the time Tom was well enough to start asking questions.

Mr Green went away to speak to the maid in person, while his wife made Sarah sit down and tell her her tragic story. As ever, Sarah's inventiveness rose to the occasion. The tale she told was harrowing even to her own ears. Mrs Green looked fit to cry.

Eventually the maid came in to conduct Sarah upstairs to the bathroom. It proved to be a luxurious apartment, with a carpet and drapes and things one didn't associate with bathrooms. It was brilliantly lighted, with many mirrors adding reflection to the electric light. The bath stood on a raised pedestal in the centre of the room. It was filled and waiting for her. The tempting water was pale green and gave off a delicious aroma.

The maid went out, leaving on a little table some clothes for Sarah to try afterwards. She undressed slowly, looking at herself in each of the mirrors in turn, striking and holding exotic poses. When she was naked she repeated the poses, pouted her lips sensuously at her reflection, and, in one of the mirrors, watched herself slowly and gracefully enter the bath.

'Where've you been?' Thomas demanded from the bed when she came in, late that afternoon.

'Shoppin',' was all the answer she gave. 'Thought we'd have a nice supper. Build up your strength.'

She placed on the table the big brown paper bag in which she had carried groceries, some steak and kidney, and a bottle of cheap port wine. She came over and gave him a kiss. He noticed how nice she smelt, and how pink and radiant she looked. Had he seen the rumpled guise in which she had gone out, he would have been even more surprised by the transformation. Her hair was immaculately done, her clothes had been pressed, the soiled blouse she had been wearing had been replaced by a crisp fresh one. She had returned by omnibus. This time, people – men especially – *had* looked at her, but had recognised anything but the Poor Young Widow of Peckham about her.

'Just shopping?' Thomas repeated. 'I don't believe you.'

'Suit yourself.'

'Course, you don't *have* to tell me. It's just that, lying here all these hours, helpless, thinking my thoughts . . .'

It was not like Thomas Watkins to give way to self-pity. The effects of his illness, no doubt.

'What thoughts, love?' she humoured him, sitting on the bed and taking his hand.

'When you've been to the brink, as I have, you get a clear picture of things. It's like you're up there in space, looking down at the world from another planet. You see your life spread out – triumphs and disasters.'

'What did you see me like? Triumph, or a disaster?'

'I'm being serious, Sarah. For once, if you like. See, I made a vow. I promised if I was spared I'd stop chasing rainbows. Find some steady work and live different.'

'I put in a word for you with old Warboils.'

'Who's he?'

'At the *Daily Mail*. When I went to collect the prize

money.' She wished she hadn't referred to that, and rattled on. 'Said you was the bloomin' cat's whiskers as a photographer. Told him he ought to snap you up before any of the others did.'

'What others?' Thank heaven, this had diverted his curiosity from the prize money.

'Well, I reckoned there was bound to be some offers, by the time you was up and about again. Aren't there any in them letters?'

She gestured towards the accumulation of post, strewn beside the bed. Thomas shook his head. 'It's the Poor Widow they're all interested in, never mind who took her picture. Anyway, I wouldn't be a press photographer if they offered. Working all hours of the day and night, living off human grief, disaster . . . I tell you, it's a humbling moment when you stand on the brink and see your true place in the cosmic scheme of things.'

'I think you're getting too deep, Tom. That's not your style.'

'My style's going to be a changed one from now on, you'll see. Tell you what I'm going to do, for a start. I've been thinking of poor old Dooley.'

'Who?'

'Next bed to me in the infirmary. I've been seeing his face while I lie here, and I thought of other faces in that place. Well, I've got a gift for faces, I've proved, so as soon as I've got my strength back I'm going down there and get permission to take pictures of old Dooley and some of the rest of them. I'll make up an album of 'em. Instead of famous last words it'll be famous last expressions. All human suffering. That's a theme worthy of my gift, 'stead of the sort of thing they'd make me do on a newspaper.'

It didn't quite sound like the steady employment he had vowed. All the same, Sarah was moved. He had proved he could do it, with his photo of her. He deserved to be given his chance.

'Look, love,' she said impulsively, 'you give it a go, and I'll take care of the rent and food while you're trying.'

He looked at her sharply. 'How? You sure you only been shopping?'

'Well, not only. See, one of the women who wrote in about the Widow offered this little job – just temporary. I thought I'd best take it, just . . . just in case anything happened to you. I know you're back, and going to be all right, but I'd promised her, so I'm starting tomorrow. It's only for a week.'

'What sort of job?'

'Dental receptionist. Very respectable establishment, only just a bus ride away. It's a favour, really, while somebody's away on holiday.'

'How much?'

'Oh, too superior to talk actual money. But it'll be more than fair, and a good meal thrown in, so we can spend it all on you.'

'Well . . .' Thomas said doubtfully.

'Never mind "well". That's what you're goin' to get. I got some nice steak and kid. to be going on with. And some port wine. Come on, I'll open the bloomin' bottle now. Celebrate the recovery of Professor Thomas B. (for Bleedin') Watkins, Photographer Exraordinary of Peckham!'

It was a week before Tom was strong enough to go back to the hospital. He took the camera and tripod with him on spec, but met with a reception somewhat less rapturous than anticipated.

'Good heavens, we don't allow that sort of thing!' he was told by Sister Teresa.

'I don't think you quite understand, Sister. It's a mission of gratitude – to take some pictures of your Trojan and devoted work. See, I can get you a lot of public sympathy. Political support, even. Perhaps money to improve facilities . . .'

'Mr Watkins, it is very well meant of you, no doubt, but our belief is that God, in His infinite mercy, will provide for us sufficiently.'

'Oh, well . . .' It was beyond Thomas to propose that he

might have been impelled to come by God, as His agent. He prepared to pick up his gear and go; but at that moment a familiar figure came in sight.

'Nurse Cecilia,' the Sister called. 'You remember Mr Watkins. See how well he's looking, after your care.'

The pretty young nun came smiling to Thomas and shook his hand. Then her expression changed to sadness.

'Have you come to see your friend Mr Dooley, Mr Watkins?'

'Well, amongst other things. I thought I'd say hello, like.'

'I'm sorry to say he passed away early this morning. His heart, you know. He slipped by quite peacefully.'

'Oh . . . well . . . I'm glad for him, then . . .'

'But he did leave a message for you, so it is as well you've called.'

'Me?'

Sister Teresa left them together. The nurse reached into her apron pocket and brought out a key and a piece of paper.

'Just this,' she told Thomas. 'And he wanted me to tell you . . .'

It was the last day of Sarah's work, but she was not yet back home when Thomas came in. He would have gone straight to the address mentioned by Nurse Cecilia as part of Arthur Dooley's final message, but for being encumbered with the photographic equipment he had not been allowed to use at the hospital. He decided to wait for her. He erected the tripod in the middle of the floor and placed the camera on it; then went to lie on the bed, to let his artistic fancies float freely, while he turned and turned the late Arthur Dooley's key in his trouser pocket.

Sarah, meanwhile, was bidding farewell to Mr and Mrs Green, of Denmark Hill.

'You've been so co-operative, my dear,' Mrs Green told her. 'Hasn't she, Hector?'

'Oh, most, most.'

'We'd ask you to stay on, but we appreciate that you have your other commitment. However, if you would like to come back again at any time . . . ?'

'Well, it depends,' Sarah said warily.

'I hope you'll agree the money has been quite satisfactory?'

'Oh, most. I reely am grateful.'

'No need at all. You have most exceptional talents. Hasn't she, Hector?'

'Oh yes. Decidedly.'

Just for once, Sarah noticed, Mr Green responded with real enthusiasm. His wife turned to glance sharply at him. Sarah seized the opportunity to throw him a broad wink. He winked back openly. Mrs Green saw him, and turned to Sarah with a smile.

'We have your address,' she said. 'We'll get in touch, shall we, when we can use you for a week, a day?'

'Well,' Sarah said, 'now that my brother-in-law's so much better, I think I might be going with him to live with my late husband's family, in the country. They've been pressing me for some time. Berkshire, you know.'

'Ah, well, jolly good for you.' It was Mr Green who surprisingly spoke. 'It's been nice, though. Very nice.'

'I bet it has! thought Sarah, as she took her leave of her benefactors and hurried for an omnibus to get her home.

Thomas was waiting impatiently. He told her to keep her outdoor things on, showed her Dooley's key, and bustled her out to walk to the address in Camberwell which had formed part of the last message passed on to him by Nurse Cecilia. Sarah walked obediently. They could well have afforded a cab, out of the money reposing in her purse. She thought it best not to volunteer one, though. Better for him to think that his prize money was still intact, and to believe that what little she had made from her temporary work had just gone far enough to pay for the extra food and drink to restore him.

Their destination proved to be a garage in a greasy alley.

Just for a moment, Sarah thought that Fate might be bringing them round full circle. In there, when Tom had finished fiddling with the key and had got the stuck old lock open. they would find the Rolls Silver Ghost awaiting them, their magic chariot restored. But the door was open at last, and there seemed to be nothing at all, save some broken bits of furniture, a dismantled brass bed, and a box or two. There was something else in a corner, shrouded in cloth. The place smelt disused and none too dry.

'Crafty old devil!' Tom was grumbling. 'Probably owes back rent on the place and wants to land it on someone else, so his Estate won't have to pay it.'

'Ask me,' Sarah responded, 'he had about as much Estate as you. Let's see what's under that cloth. If there's nothing, we're goin', and no more questions asked.'

Thomas went across and whisked the cloth aside, revealing a pin-table football game of a type she had seen in fun fairs and, most recently, on Brighton pier during their brief idyll there.

'Cor!' Sarah exclaimed. 'Remember that? One at Brighton owes you two bob.'

'Look at this!' He had drawn back the cloth further. There was another table, a clown's hat game, in as good condition as the other.

'What's it all add up to?' she asked, peering.

'Simple enough,' he answered smugly. 'Wanted me to have his possessions, and these are them. Gratitude of someone bequeathing all he had in the world to "an artist who'd made the nation look its conscience in the face". Those were his last words, Nurse said. Got a penny on you? See if they still work.'

Sarah was glad to be able to hand over a penny. It would have been awkward having to explain that, otherwise, she had nothing smaller than pound notes.

The note which Arthur Dooley had left for Thomas was legal authorisation enough for him to have the machines removed to a fun arcade in Tottenham Court Road, whose owner he had talked into accommodating them for a share of their takings.

'Sixty-forty in his bleedin' favour!' Sarah expostulated yet again, as they went there one evening three weeks later to collect the pay-out. But Thomas gave her a reassuring pat on the shoulder. He was fully recovered now. There was no more talk of Higher Intentions or cosmic planes; only of even greater expectations, this week than the six pounds twelve-and-sixpence the games had made for them in their first week's operation. So flush was he feeling that he had never even called for a full accounting from her of his photographic prize money. It would not have troubled her if he had; the full twenty-five pounds was intact, and she had a little additional hoard of her own.

'Sixty-forty!' she complained, nevertheless.

'Never mind, love. They have to make their money, and we don't have to work for ours any more. By the way, I've decided to flog the camera and stuff, so you can have a bath when you want.'

'Get rid of the camera? What about your album of all human sufferin', then?'

'Well, see, I was thinking it over, and it seemed to me that it would be wrong for an artist to take pecuniary advantage of others less fortunate. I mean, it's one thing to make a few quid from a faked-up picture like I took of you – and do a bit of good with it on the side – but to exploit those who are down . . . What are you looking at?'

They had entered the fun fair. It was Sarah's first visit there. She saw at a glance that their own two machines had been given a good position in the centre of the garish hall, and was pleased to note a group of sharply dressed youths round each, clattering coins into the slots and groaning with disappointment as they lost them for ever. What had really attracted her attention, though, was a machine at the side, and the little queue of older men waiting to use it.

WHAT THE BUTLER SAW, its painted title proclaimed; but on its front was pasted a cardboard notice: 'New this week: CAUGHT IN THE BATH!'

'Nothin',' Sarah answered quickly, but he had followed her gaze. He snorted contemptuously.

'Take that sort of thing, for instance. Know what those sort of people do? Pick up women who're down on their luck and give 'em a quid or two to pose in the altogether. Call that photography? I'd sooner starve than have any hand in that.'

As indeed, she thought as they went past, you might have done, if you'd been ill a long time, and the prize money had run out, and old Irvine had had your camera and everything else, and you'd come home to nothin' at all, instead of to meat, and veg., and port wine.

Filthy old pair, she had thought of Mr and Mrs Green, when she'd heard that strange sound from outside the bathroom, a sort of whirring and cranking, and suddenly twigged that the aperture in the wall, and all that bright lighting, were to do with photography, and that she was the subject.

'Not *that* sort of picture,' Tom had assured her, when he had first hinted that she should be his model. Well, he had come up trumps with his poetic vision, or whatever it was he'd called it, and nearly died as a result. And as soon as she had got over the shock of realising what the Greens were using her for, she had seen the ironic side, and played up for them in a way that had shown them she knew their game. So, after that first session, she had bluntly stated her terms for carrying on through the week.

'I think we might well be able to agree to that,' Mrs Green had smiled. 'Don't you, Hector?'

'Of course, dear,' he had assented, puffing his pipe as unconcernedly as if she had asked if he would mind ginger pudding again instead of the treacle.

They had not gone so far as to show her the results of her work before paying her off. But, from the daily and prolonged bath she had agreed to take, and the entrance each time of the maid, Grace, to soap her back and then drape her in discreet towels when she rose to emerge, Sarah knew pretty well now what was being seen by the eyes glued to the eyepiece of that fun fair machine and perhaps others all over the place. And as she urged an oblivious Thomas through into the proprietor's office, she was thankful, for once, that no one in that fun fair had given her a second glance.

CHAPTER FIVE

'I reckon,' Thomas remarked one morning, as they lay side by side in bed, too comfortable to be bothered getting up, 'that we've made enough to book ourselves a room in some rather lovely hotel.'

'Oh, yes!' was Sarah's eager response. the obvious vision of the Brighton Metropole was instantly before her eyes. 'If we ask 'em, we can probably get the same room as last time.'

'Ah, but I'm afraid you haven't quite got my drift. I wasn't referring to that sort of hotel at all. I had in mind more the kind that floats.'

'Come again?'

'Remember that poster I had of the S.S. *Olympic*, on the wall of our place in Kilburn? How I said we'd make that Atlantic crossing ourselves, some day?'

'Yeh. And I said we'd need to make a fortune first.'

'Well, we haven't exactly a fortune yet; but there's a tidy little bit put by, and a regular income coming from the machines. Now's the time to accelerate a bit. Push down on the throttle and speed up. There's nowhere like the 'States for getting on fast.'

Sarah moved her head to stare at him. 'You're not serious, Tom?'

'Course I'm serious. No need to wait years to make a fortune here, when we can do it in a tenth of the time over there.'

'What . . . what line of business would you go into?'

'Can't say, till I get there and take a good look round. See, there was this Scottish family who went, in about 1850. Poor as church mice. The father was a weaver, his wife sewed shoes. Their little boy went to work in a cotton factory. Then he was a telegraph clerk, then secretary to a railway boss. But he looked a lot further ahead than that. He saw how important steel was going to be in the world, and he got himself into that line. He ended up with a monopoly of all the steel in America, and the government had to buy him out. D'you know how much they had to pay?'

'Search me. Best part of a million, I suppose.'

'Two hundred and fifty million dollars. *Two hundred and fifty million.* That's what I mean by a fortune, like Andrew Carnegie made. And there's only one place in the world to pull it off.'

'You don't know anything about steel.'

'More than you think. Anyway, I'm not talking about the steel business for me. I'll find something else. Something no one's cottoned on to yet. So simple and obvious that they'll all be kicking themselves for not getting on to it first, while I'll be laughing all the way to the bank. Yes, I reckon my mind's just about made up.'

The exciting vision had provoked his impatience. He had at present no calls on his time, other than to go to the fun arcade once a week and pick up the profits; but his thoughts had made him too restless to go on lying there in bed. He went out to the bathroom to get shaved.

Sarah remained where she was. She was comfortable not only in the bed but in her circumstances in general. For once they had a decent steady income. They had been able to give up the drab room over the pawnbroker's and move here to the North London suburb of Finchley, where everything was clean, even the air. They had taken a bed-sittingroom over a delicatessen shop owned by a Hungarian-born couple little older than Sarah's twenty-seven years. Their intention was to look for a proper flat in this agreeable district, and Thomas, who had been at his most amiable since coming into modest money, had sensibly suggested that they ought to lodge there first and take their time about searching around.

The room was a great improvement on the last, with its own kitchen and bathroom as separate apartments, a nice double bed and other furnishings. Sarah liked it so much that she wouldn't even have minded staying on. It was cheap and needed little work. The only feature she didn't like was the curtains, which were of a colour she had never been able to stick. With the permission of their friendly landlady, she had just bought some others of her own choosing. Mrs Zvovovski had said she would come up this afternoon, which was half-day closing, and help her hang them.

And now, here was Tom threatening her peace of mind all over again with another of his big ideas. Such security as Sarah felt with him was a frail enough thing at best. He still had made no offer to marry her, and she had stopped herself from bringing up the subject, for fear of spoiling the contented peace of these last few weeks. She knew him too well to imagine that he would be content for long to live off the proceeds from the amusement arcade. She was quite ready to play her part in some new enterprise which might just strike lucky. If it failed, and their savings went, at least there was still the steady income; she would try to draw the line at his putting that into hock. But, at the very worst, she could fall back on her own resources, such as a return to the halls, or some more modelling for Mr and Mrs Green, with domestic service as the last resort of all.

Sarah was certain she could cope with anything while she remained in the familiar surroundings of her native London, or even elsewhere in England. But in a foreign place, all them thousands of miles away – dread began to rise in her and her heart pounded. When Tom was nice, he was very, very nice; and security seemed to be the thing that kept him that way. But in the longer term she knew there was a limit to the degree she could trust him. She could easily envisage a situation in which, once landed in America, he would go chasing off on some madcap scheme, leaving her to fend for herself until he came back rich. With his sharp wits he might even succeed; but she was sure that old Carnegie, or whatever his name was, hadn't made his milions overnight. Neither would Tom Watkins, and Sarah feared the circumstances under which she would have to wait.

She mentioned the possibility to Mrs Zvovovski as they

worked together on the curtains that afternoon. Tom had gone out for a game of snooker at a public hall off Finchley High Street.

'Stoff!' the Hungarian woman snorted. 'You don't vont to go vonting to go to America.'

'I don't, Mrs Zvovovski. It's all Tom's idea.'

'It's Stoff. And its time you calling me Janine. Six weeks you are lodging here.'

Sarah smiled gratefully. 'The trouble is, once Tom sets his heart on something . . . Honest, I'd be quite content to settle for something like you got here – a nice little shop of your own, a place to live. That'd be enough for me.'

'You're right, my dear. Places like this is improving all the time. You know, ven Milos and me makes enough money in the East End to move out here, this place has no pastry shop. Ve vos the first. Now, vis Hampstead Garden Suburb growing joost round the corner, and many Jewish coming to live, there is delicatessen all over the place. But Milos and me vos the first, and all our customers coming regular and recommending.'

Sarah sighed. She knew that the Zvovovskis had emigrated without a bean in their pockets and were now far richer than their small shop might suggest.

'Well,' she said, 'I suppose you and Mr Zvovovski took a chance on a foreign country, and it came off.'

'Ve had no other chance. Ve had to get out. But you, you got no need. I tell you this – ve could have gone to America, 'stead of coming here. Ve give thanks all the time for how ve decide.'

'Tom says it's the Land of Golden Opportunity.'

'Stoff! My Oncle Sandor and Aunt Gizelle is gone to America. He is beautiful tailor. You know vot he has to do? He has to cut out silhouettes of President Roosevelt and sell in street. A tailor who can cut suits vith the best, he cuts out paper silhouettes. My Aunt Gizelle is seamstress. Beautiful vorks, You know vot she does? She hems table cloths at ten cents a time. That's vot you get in America, my dear. You listen to Janine, and stay right vere you is.'

She stepped down the small ladder and surveyed the newly-hung curtains.

'There! Is pretty. You comfortable. You stay.'

Sarah relayed the burden of this advice to Thomas when he came home. She was alarmed to see brochures about travel to America in his hand.

'And,' she added, 'there's all sorts of restrictions. You got anything wrong with you and they keep you on a thing called Ellis Island, till they can ship you out again. Janine says you got to have your marriage lines all legal, too – not that I let on we wasn't hitched proper.'

Thomas grinned smugly. 'There's nothing wrong with either of us. And as we're single there's nothing to stop us going in separately and getting together again after. There's a way round everything in this world.'

The very slight hope Sarah had begun to entertain that this might turn out to be the one thing that would persuade him to marry her faded. She fell back on pleading.

'We don't have to go to America to get on, Tom. There must be opportunities here, when you've got a bit of money behind you. And if we took a little shop like Janine's, with somewhere cosy like this over it to live, I'd have plenty to do and I wouldn't mind how much you wanted to go off chasing about making your pile. You could use all the cash from the machines, and . . .'

'Listen, there's just this big difference between the 'States and here. Over there, they want you to be successful. Here, they want to keep you in your place, which is bottom of the heap. I'm going to be rich by I'm forty, not punch-drunk from trying.' He returned to the study of his brochures.

Sarah took a deep breath. His implacability left her no choice but to play her one trump card. If it still wasn't enough to win her the game, she had decided, she would simply tell him to go alone and leave her to fend for herself. She didn't want to: but, even more, she was determined not to be dragged to America.

'Hey ho!' she sighed. 'Then we go, and that's it. So, here's wishing good luck to the three of us.'

'Three? You planning on taking someone else along?'

'Ain't got much choice, have I? Still, as you say, there's a way round everything. I dare say you can wangle it for 'em to let me in, and perhaps it would be a better start in America for a baby.'

Thomas sat up. 'A baby? You mean you're pregnant again?'

'Hardly be expectin' a baby if I wasn't.'

He leaped to his feet, letting the brochures slide unheeded to the floor.

'Then why the bloody hell didn't you say so in the first place? Now you tell me, when I've got it all planned.'

She answered in a small voice, 'I only found out this afternoon. I'd been wonderin', and I don't know the doctors round here, so I went over Kilburn way to see Dr Gordon. You remember him? I never minded him messing about with me. He wished us better luck this time. Tom, it's not that I don't *want* to go to America. It's just that, well, might be third time lucky, if I can hang on to this one.'

She would have expected no congratulation from him even in better circumstances, and certainly got none now. He lit a cigarette and paced about the little room, the dark eyes dulled and his mouth turned down.

'I'm truly sorry,' she added, knowing she mustn't overdo it.

'It's all right, girl.' His tone was as dull as his look.

'I mean, I know how much you was lookin' forward to going.'

'Do you? I doubt it.'

'Course' – this was a risky one – 'you could go on your own, and we could come out after you.'

She held her breath, seeing him pause to think about it; but he said leadenly, 'It's all right, Sarah. We'll stay.'

She could afford now to give him back some of his hope.

'Tell you what – we'll get a little shop, like we was saving, to tide us over and make a bit more money to put by. Then as soon as I've had the baby, out we go – eh?'

Thomas threw the cigarette into the empty grate. He stooped down for the brochures and dismissively threw them after it. Sarah breathed freely again, with uneasy relief.

The shop they found through a newspaper advertisement was at Mortlake, a prosperous, busy suburb on the south bank of the Thames, where it described a great loop between Richmond and Putney. They had looked at one or two places in North London, where Sarah would have preferred to have stayed, but they had proved either too expensive or unsuitable for other reasons. The range from which they could choose was also limited by the bounds of their joint experience. Thomas had no taste for a return to engineering or garage ownership; he insisted on something at which he could keep his hands clean and wear decent clothes. He was not going to have the label 'Trade' hung round his neck, except while he was behind the counter.

'No one's going to make jokes about me being "Watkins the Dairy",' he declared, referring to the proliferation of little dairies-cum-groceries kept by Welsh families in every district of London.

They settled for the drapery and haberdashery, with a view of the river from its upstairs window. It was nothing grand, but had a genteel atmosphere to it which pleased Sarah. She had toiled in a garment sweatshop in her girlhood, so it was nice to sell products of that kind to the good class of customers who would have no inkling of the sordid background to their manufacture. Her good taste in clothes stood her in good stead, too. Displaying no ill will over the American disappointment, Thomas threw himself into the business with customary fluency, treating their customers more as equals than superiors and pleasing the spinster ladies with his Welsh good looks and charm.

'My word, Miss Jenkins, if I may say so you're looking

quite blooming today. That grenadine looks like pure silk, the way you wear it.'

The customer, middle-aged, and painfully shy, accepted the chair he had come round the counter to proffer her. She blushed deeply, and wondered whether it was quite right for them to be outside the counter together without Mrs Watkins present in the shop.

'Now,' he said, returning behind the stockade, 'there's a most attractive new pattern book just come in. I thought to myself, I'm sure Miss Jenkins would like to be the first to look at it, so I've kept it under the counter here.'

Miss Jenkins wagged a finger. 'Now, now, Mr Watkins, you mustn't tempt me. I'm in sufficient trouble already.'

'Trouble, Miss Jenkins? Don't tell me your mother didn't like the brocade.'

'She liked it very much, but I got a scolding for buying it. I'm afraid my trouble is my inability to resist your very persuasive sales talk.'

'The only way to avoid it will be to stop coming in here, Miss Jenkins – in which case, I shall never be able to face my poor little wife again for having driven away her favourite customer. But since you are here, even if it is for the last time, perhaps you would care to see the new patterns, just in case you can't find them anywhere else?'

'Mr Watkins, you are incorrigible. I shall tell Mrs Watkins so when I see her next. Is she well?'

'Blooming, thank you. She's putting some finishing touches to our flat. A natural home-maker. Now, here's the book. You just sit there comfy and take all afternoon if you wish.'

While this coy exchange was going on Sarah was hanging curtains again. She had brought the pretty ones from Finchley, but had only just found time to alter them. Drawn that evening, with the electric light making them glow, they looked like a theatre drop, reaching all the way to the floor and giving the little sitting-room a taller appearance. Sarah kept glancing at them from her chair, where she sat sewing. Thomas occupied a hard chair at the table. He was entering up the twin ledgers, automatically refreshing himself with beer.

'This is the life,' Sarah sighed, more to herself than him.

'For some, maybe,' he answered, without looking up. It startled her. She had thought he was quite enjoying it, too.

'Haven't heard you exactly complaining,' she responded cautiously.

'Haven't had much chance, have I? Not with you constantly extolling the wonderful virtues of a settled, stable and respectable existence.' He put down his pen and turned on his chair to face her. She was relieved to note that he was looking cheerful enough.

'You know,' he went on, 'once, I'd never have put that down to you, wanting to be stable and respectable . . .'

'And married,' she risked reminding him.

'One thing at a time, Sarah.'

'You did promise.'

'You promised to go to America.'

'We'll go.'

'Like we'll get married.'

'Thomas Watkins, there are times when I hate you.'

'Just as well we're not married, then.'

'Huh! Fat chance I've got, anyway. You're bleedin' married already – to your bank account.'

'Only weeks since you was saying I was married to Elsie – the camera, remember?'

'Oh, her. You chucked her over, like you would anything else you didn't have no more use for.'

'I see. So it's the bank account you're jealous of now. Always has to be something. Of course, you yourself have no interest whatsoever in money.'

'At least when I can't sleep I don't count the day's takings in my head, instead of sheep.'

'In that case, I'd be wasting my breath telling you this week's profits I just worked out. I mean, you wouldn't be interested to know we'd made . . .' He paused deliberately, teasing her by peering close at the open ledger and whistling with astonishment. She took the bait.

'How much?'

'You don't want to know.'

'Course I bleedin' do. Come on!'

'Thirty-two pound.'

Her big eyes grew enormous. 'Thirty-two quid!'

'That's net, not gross. All profit. But, of course, it'll have bored you so much that you'll be falling out of your chair any time now.'

She returned him a grin and mimed doing so.

'Right,' she declared. 'Before you finish off the figures you can deduct the price of a new hat.'

He eyed her levelly. 'There's nothing you need a new hat for, Sarah. We're building up our savings, remember?'

Muttering something indecent about the scope of the mean habits of Welshmen, she went back to her sewing. Thomas picked up his pen and ruler and drew a firm line under his final figure.

She got her own back on him next morning, however. Determined to get herself a new look, she took one of the stage hats from the property skip down into the shop, and experimented on it with various accessories. It was lying on the counter before her when the door bell jingled and the first customer of the day entered. She was Mrs Ryder, the vicar's wife. Like the other ladies of her husband's parish she had shown herself susceptible to Thomas's charm.

'Good morning, Mr Watkins. Good morning, Mrs Watkins. Isn't it a gorgeous morning?'

'Indeed, indeed,' answered Thomas, who hadn't really noticed. 'My word, that's excellent lace, Mrs Ryder. Mechlin? No, Roman Point. Exquisite. And how is Mr Ryder? Miss Jenkins was saying he had a very bad cold.'

'Oh well, yes, but it makes no difference. Rushed off his feet as usual, poor soul. Two funerals and a Churching today. Four weddings, no less, on Saturday, as well as all the preparations for the bishop's visit. Which reminds me . . .'

She broke off. Her eye had fallen upon the hat. Sarah

noticed her mouth twitch, as if she had had to stop herself licking her lips.

'Yes, Mrs Ryder?' Thomas prompted.

'Oh, er, yes. We're having a little sherry morning after Matins this Sunday, to celebrate the bishop's visit, you understand, and my husband and I would be delighted if you could both come.'

Sarah accepted too quickly for Thomas's liking. He added more decorously, '*We* should be delighted, Mrs Ryder.'

'Splendid! You've already made quite an impression on our little community in the short time you've been here. Perhaps we may see you in church soon?'

'No perhaps about it,' Thomas assured her. 'It's been a question of getting properly settled in, you know. Not much time except Sundays so far.'

'I quite understand, Mr Watkins. Well, that's what I really came into say to you.' Her eyes were on the hat again. 'But . . . I know I shouldn't, but I *was* thinking of buying a new hat for Sunday. I wonder . . .'

Sarah opened her mouth but this time Thomas spoke first.

'If I may say so, Mrs Ryder, your timing is immaculate. If you hadn't come in with your kind invitation, this original creation would have been in the window by now. We were just saying that we didn't expect it to stay there long – even at the price.'

Mrs Ryder swallowed. 'How . . . how much is it?' she almost whispered.

Ten minutes later, having tried it on and being praised to the skies by Thomas, she left with the hat.

'"Original creation" indeed!' Sarah exclaimed. 'And that price!'

'So what? I've made her happy. She didn't look half bad in it, and she'll tell everyone where she got it.'

'Right – then I want my commission.'

'What are you talking about? It was lying there in the skip, doing nothing.'

'It's what I'd done to it that caught her eye – them cherries and things. I've got artistic bloomin' vision, too, you know. Come on – half thirty-five bob's seventeen-and-a-tanner. Hand over!'

He pulled a wry face, but obeyed. So both Mrs Ryder and Sarah had new hats to be proud of on Sunday morning. Thomas shrewdly suggested to Sarah that they should go to Matins, and be well seen; it would make things that much easier all round at the reception afterwards. Sarah was not at all averse to dressing up and showing herself off to Mr Ryder's congregation. She was gratified to notice from the corners of her eyes, as they walked gravely along the aisle, people glancing in their direction and heads being bent together as explanations were made.

'Hope no one saw you asleep during the sermon,' she told Thomas as they made their way towards the vicarage afterwards.

'I wasn't asleep. I was withdrawn in deep contemplation.'

'I had to nudge you twice from snoring. Anyway, it's quite a thing to get you into a church at all. I thought you was meant to be a Methodist.'

'I'm an Opportunist. Not so much a religion, like, as a persuasion. Here we are. And we take no snubs from anyone, remember. We're Thomas Watkins *Esquire*, and his lady.'

As it happened, people proved to be most friendly.

'Edward,' Mrs Ryder said to her husband, bringing him over to meet them, 'Mr Watkins was just being most complimentary about your sermon.'

'That so? Most pleased to hear it, sir. I've always thought people use the time to catch up on lost sleep.'

'Not at all, vicar. A masterly discourse. Most provocative.'

'Really? I hadn't realised. Any part in particular?'

'The conclusion. "All the rivers run into the sea, yet the sea is not full."' Sarah stared at him. He was a constant source of surprise to her. The vicar was looking most pleased. Her arm was taken by Mrs Ryder and the two hats went side by side towards a group of ladies.

'My dear, you know Miss Jenkins already. And Miss Fossett. I was saying to Miss Fossett just a moment ago, we don't know how we ladies managed before your most welcome arrival. Your predecessors at your shop were terribly old-fashioned. Ah, here comes Mrs White, whom you know. And Mrs Bradley-Norton – I'm not sure whether you have met Mrs Watkins, Mrs Bradley-Norton? She and her husband have taken the draper's and haberdasher's in the High Street.'

'That's right,' Sarah said. 'I don't think I've seen you in our shop, though, Mrs Bradley.'

'Bradley-*Norton*. I do not go into shops.'

Miss Jenkins put in hastily, 'Mrs Bradley-Norton lives in Bridge House, Mrs Watkins. The big white house, down by the river.'

'Oh yes,' Sarah answered easily. 'Sorry, Mrs Bradley-Norton. Of course, your maid would do all your shopping for you.'

'That is correct.'

'Mm.' Sarah took quick note of the material and the colour of the dress being worn by this sudden adversary. 'Forgive me asking, Mrs Bradley-Norton, but do you know how much crêpe de chine costs per yard?'

'I most certainly do,' came the confident reply from the formidable lady. 'Crêpe de chine is approximately nine shilling and sixpence a yard.'

'*Five* and six,' Sarah corrected her. 'That's it, you see. These girls, maids and the like, they don't half like to get the chance of fiddling their employers. You see, we've got this girl Rosie Meadows helping us now. Bit wet behind the ears, so she don't know what these maids is up to, coming in with orders and asking for more to be put on the bills than the real cost. That, and over-ordering the material needed. You know, I wouldn't be surprised at all if you find someone in your household wearing a pretty little blouse made up in lavender crêpe de chine on her day off. Dreadful what these girls get up to. I must have a word with Rosie as soon as I get back. Make her *au fait* with the wicked ways of the world.'

She nodded grandly and wandered away, leaving Mrs Bradley-Norton stranded and the other ladies much impressed.

Rosie Meadows was indeed inexperienced and young; but she was willing. With her in the shop to do as Sarah told her, and especially the lifting, Thomas felt freer to go out and about on what he termed 'men's business', consisting largely of playing snooker and placing bets on horses. Once he had asserted this freedom he largely ceased to bother telling Sarah where he was off to, or when he would be back.

'Here, Mrs Watkins,' Rosie remonstrated a few days later, 'you oughtn't to be doing that – stretching your hands up for them boxes, in your condition. You know what Mr Watkins warned.'

'Oh, yeh,' said Sarah, relinquishing the task to her. 'Talking of which, any idea where my husband's gone today?'

'Oh, I forgot to tell you. He went out soon after we'd opened up. He said I was to tell you he was off over to Kilburn.'

'Kilburn?' A little stab of alarm pricked Sarah. 'What for?'

'Something to do with a garridge he once had there. Bloke sent a message to say he'd found some tools belonging to Mr Watkins, and if he wanted 'em would he come and get 'em straightaway, 'cos the place has been sold again.'

Sarah regarded her. 'When did this message come?'

'Just this morning. Mr Watkins went off with the bloke, as he was going back that way in a van.'

'I see.'

'He said he'd be back for his dinner, and he was going to get his hair cut while he's there.'

Sarah smiled. Tom had always declared that club-footed

Max at Kilburn was the best barber north of the Thames. The fact that he had troubled to leave her a message was reassurance enough that she had no reason to be suspicious about his purpose in revisiting Kilburn.

CHAPTER SIX

'I said to myself as you walked in, "It's Mr Watkins, as I live and breathe." And how are you keeping, sir?'

Max beamed at Thomas's reflection in the mirror as he whisked the white gown around him and tucked it in at the neck.

'Never better, thanks, Max. I was in the area – business, you know – and south of the river they don't cut hair like you do, so I thought I'd look in.'

'I take that to be a compliment, sir; I take that to be a compliment. So that's where you are now – south of the river?'

'Mortlake, actually.'

'Oh, very select, sir. Very select. Missus and I always go to watch the Boat Race, and it's the finishing line at Mortlake we make for, because it's such a nice part. Short back and sides and a shave, sir?'

'As usual. And nothing about the weather.'

'I like that, sir; I like that.' The little barber bustled about his trade. There were no other customers in the clean, shining shop. Max's young assistant was absorbed in a racing paper.

'You're in the garage business at Mortlake, Mr Watkins?'

'Not now. Got a little chain of shops these days. Drapery and haberdashery.'

'Nice line of business, sir. High class trade in that part, of course.'

'Oh, very high. Vicars' wives, double-barrelled ladies . . .'

'I like that, sir. "Double-barrelled ladies"!'

The little man's laughter was interrupted by the entrance of another customer, whose face caused him to exclaim, 'Well, if it isn't Dr Gordon, as I live and breathe. That's two old customers in a morning. How are you, Doctor, sir?'

'Very well, thanks, Max,' replied the athletic-looking young doctor, whose skin bore a fine suntan.

'Do you want to wait, sir, or will you take Jack? He's a good boy, is Jack.'

The doctor smiled. 'I'll take Jack, then.' He nodded to Thomas but appeared not to recognise him from the old days.

'See, Jack,' Max was saying proudly, 'when you get old customers coming back, you know you got a reputation. Did you know Mr Watkins, Doctor? He had the garage that used to be poor Jack Fellows's. You attended him in his last illness, didn't you?'

'Ah, yes, I remember. Sorry, Mr Watkins, I can't place you, though. So many patients, you understand.'

'Well,' Thomas smiled across to him in the other chair, 'talking of old customers coming back, you got one just a few weeks ago. My wife, Sarah.'

The doctor returned him a puzzled look. Max broke in, 'I forgot to ask after the missus, Mr Watkins. How is she keeping?'

'You could ask the doctor that, Max. It's no secret. She's in the family way again.'

'Well, congrat . . .' the barber began, but halted in mid-word, looking puzzled. He looked across to Dr Gordon, whose expression was similarly surprised.

'Good news, Mr Watkins,' the doctor said, 'but I'm afraid it didn't come from me.'

'But it must . . . You remember Sarah, don't you?'

'Very well. I'm very pleased for her.'

'Ah, I understand. With all your rush of patients, you couldn't be expected to recall a single visit amongst 'em. No, of course.'

'I don't think you understand,' the doctor replied pleasantly. 'As Max here could tell you, I was offered a cruise as ship's surgeon to South Africa and back, and took the chance to stay a few months with my brother at the Cape. I only got back two days ago. What Mrs Watkins must have meant was that she was examined by my locum at my surgery; but she certainly wasn't seen by me.'

'Oh . . . !' Thomas mumbled. 'I see. Yes, I see.'

The lathered brush debarred him from speaking further. Max asked, 'And how did you find the Cape, Doctor? Very select there, I'd imagine . . .' But Thomas was no longer listening.

He was unsteady on his feet when he entered his shop later that afternoon. He brought whisky fumes in with him. Sarah said quickly, 'Rosie, look after things for a bit. I'm just going upstairs with Mr Watkins.'

She followed him, noting how much he relied upon the banister rail. He regularly went out for his midday drink, but in all these last weeks she had never seen him the worse for it. And he had come back long after she had expected him. His dinner was dried up and wasted by now.

'Rosie told me you'd be back for dinner,' she said brightly when they were in their room. 'It was too long in the oven, though. How about some nice cheese and pickles, and I'll cook again this evening?'

'Don't want anything.'

'You got somethin' out, did you?'

'Never mind about bloody food. All I want's a drink.'

He crossed to the cupboard where their modest supply was kept and brought out a half-bottle of whisky, partly full.

'Seems you've had a few already,' Sarah said, her tone hardening a little.

'So I have. Met a man.'

'Oh, yes? Anyone I know?'

He had falteringly poured some of the whisky into a glass. He drank it straight down and immediately recharged the glass. There was something menacing about his recklessness.

'Anyone you know? Oh, that's funny, that is. Course you know him. You let him mess about with you.'

'*What?* There's nobody in Kilburn ever messed about

with me, Tom Watkins, so you can keep your filthy mouth to yourself! You're stinkin' drunk.'

He gave an idiotic laugh and drank his whisky. Sarah came round the table, determined to get the bottle off him. He held it up out of her reach and mocked, 'Know what I warned you 'bout reachin' and that. Got to be careful, 'n your condition.'

'You got to be careful, too. You'll kill yourself, drinkin' like that. Come on, Tom, give us the bottle.'

'I'm all right.' He assumed an innocent tone of voice. 'You got to be careful, though. Old Max asked to be 'membered to you.'

'That's nice. So's your hair. You're right, nobody does it like Max.'

'Like old times, sitting in his chair. Catch up with local gossip and that.'

'Yeh, I'll bet. Anythin' interestin'?'

He had been leading up to confronting her with her lie about having been examined by Dr Gordon. Some instinct, though, made him hold back. It would be like inflicting quick and private death on someone who deserved to suffer it drawn-out and with public humiliation,

'Not really,' he had control enough to answer instead. But he couldn't resist making the first insertion of the knife he would twist when the time came. 'Doctor came in for his shave while I was in Max's. Sent his respects, too.' He noted with savage pleasure the expression of alarm, then wariness, which this news brought to her face. He saw how she swallowed and quickly licked her lips. 'You due to go and see him again before long?'

'Oh . . . Yeh, yeh. By the way, I got some news for you, Tom. We've been invited to the Bradley-Nortons'. Musical evenin'. Seems she's grateful for somethin' I told her. It'll be a step up for us locally, won't it?'

Tom sucked his teeth. 'I dunno.'

'Course it will. Every bloomin' body fawns on her round here. If she starts giving us the good word the trade'll come flocking.'

'I meant I dunno whether we ought to accept.'

'Whyever not?'

'We got to think of your condition, that's why. Mustn't take chances this time.'

'Oh, that. I'm all right, Tom. Truly.'

'Hm. *How* far are you now? I forget.'

She licked her lips again, and there was a false ring to her laugh. 'Oh, you mean it don't show. It's like that with me. It didn't show for ages last time. But you wouldn't remember, 'cos you weren't exactly around, were you?'

She hadn't been able to resist this reference to his having deserted her when he had got her pregnant before. His eyes flashed and he almost retaliated there and then. But his control remained intact. The only pleasure to be got from his revenge would be in the public taking of it.

'All right,' he said mildly. 'If you're sure it's all right, we'll accept Mrs Bradley-Norton's invitation with pleasure.'

Bridge House, the Bradley-Norton residence, was a house of some local status for its riverside position. There was nothing historic or grand about it, however. The notion of grandeur was in Mrs Bradley-Norton's mind, manifesting itself in occasional musical evenings, with hired soloists. These were, in their way, command performances: the favour of the formidable hostess was much sought. She had bullied her way to prominence on countless social committees and the ladies found it more comfortable to keep in her good books than to risk ostracism by opposing or ignoring her. Her husband, a businessman, was pompous and aloof, with the shrewdness to maintain a background place in her society activities. The musical part of her evenings bored him; he had no more of an ear than she had. But he was generous with the refreshments, thus enabling himself to partake freely and float through the proceedings with a minimum of pain.

The false grandeur of this middle-class gathering, with everyone wearing their best, two hired servants to supplement the Bradley-Nortons' own in dispensing food and drink, and the Italian tenor posturing stiffly in front of the grand piano, was apparent to Sarah. She had seen enough of the way real gentry comported themselves during her time with the Bellamy family at Eaton Place. She knew the tenor would get and deserve the raspberry in any music hall, and his woman accompanist ought to have her head laid on the keyboard and the piano lid brought down sharply on it. But it amused her to watch the other women sucking up to Mrs B-N, and all the husbands meekly supporting them. Never mind: if a spot of sucking-up would be good for trade, she wouldn't hesitate to indulge in it herself.

Her one immediate worry, as she suffered through an excruciating rendering of Tosti's 'Good-bye!', was Thomas, occupying the chair at her side. The whiff on his breath was not the result of Mr Bradley-Norton's sherry, which was all they had had so far; it was from the whiskey he had drunk before they set out.

'Doesn't do to take chances with these do's,' he had answered when she remonstrated with him. 'Might only get one drink apiece.'

'Miss Jenkins was saying how generous they are. Says even her mother's got tiddly before now.'

'What it takes to get Mrs Jenkins tiddly isn't necessarily the same as it takes me.' And he had poured himself yet another, neat.

The last inaccurate note had died its agonising death and the audience was applauding warmly. Sarah joined in, not wishing to be seen abstaining. Thomas had no such scruples. The hired maids were picking up trays of fresh sherry glasses. He scrambled up and made haste towards one of them. He surprised the girl by seizing a glass and draining it right off, then taking another. Then he wandered away towards a little knot of people gathering around Mrs Bradley-Norton. The vicar was there, with Mrs Ryder, still proudly crowned with her hat; Miss Jenkins with her sour old mother; Miss Fossett, Mrs Gilbert . . . All the old tabbies, in fact; and Sarah.

'Ah, Mrs Bradley-Norton!' Thomas interrupted cheerily. 'What an amazing tenor.'

She beamed. 'My new protégé, Signor Bertone.'

'You don't say you actually discovered him yourself?'

'In Italy. On my travels early this year, in a small café in Positano. Wasn't I clever? An original talent, wouldn't you say?'

Several acolytes gave her the congratulations she expected.

'Most original, Mrs Bradley-Norton,' agreed the vicar, and seemed not to be indulging secret irony.

'I'd go further than that, Mrs Bradley-Norton,' Thomas went on. 'I'd say unique.'

He took another glass of sherry from a maid's tray. 'Tom . . .' Sarah said, in a low tone, at his side.

'My wife agrees with me, don't you dear?' he told the assembly in a voice that was becoming unnaturally loud. 'Very good judge of singing, is Sarah, Done a bit herself, you know.'

'How very interesting,' Mrs Bradley-Norton beamed.

'Only as an amateur, actually,' Sarah hastened to explain. 'Nothing really.'

'Too modest by far,' Thomas insisted. 'Used to sing professionally – on the halls.'

'What was that?' croaked Mrs Jenkins to her daughter, who opened her mouth and shut it again.

'The music halls, Mrs Jenkins,' Thomas answered for her, even more loudly.

At that moment Mr Bradley-Norton joined the group. His wife, perceiving that something was beginning to go wrong, hastened to introduce him. 'I don't think you've met Mr and Mrs Watkins properly, dear. My husband, Arthur.'

'Arthur!' Tom cried. He turned to Sarah. 'There you are, There's your cue for a song, if somebody can play it. "A Bleedin' Stallion is my Uncle Arthur". One of her most popular favourites,' he explained to the horrorstruck faces around him.

The vicar cleared his throat, turning to his wife: 'I think, er, dear, we should be leaving.'

'Yes,' Thomas reminisced, 'a great little singer was our Sarah. Mind you, a lot of the audience used to come just to look at her legs. Give her another drink someone, and she'll show 'em for you. Come on! Any takers, now? Vicar? Come on, old sport. Might as well take a look at the goods now, 'cos I'll be askin' you to marry 'em to me one of these days, after our kid's born . . .'

'You rotten, stinkin' bastard!' she raged, as soon as they were alone in their own apartment, to which she had precipitately run and he had staggered after. 'You realise you've gone and ruined everything for us here, don't you?'

'Whass? Whassay? I only tole truth. Never be 'shamed truth. I mean . . . pretend we're married! But we're not . . . married. So sh'n't pretend. Like f'r instance, you pr'tending be pregnant. S'shame thing.'

'Stupid, drunken bastard!'

'Nor'tall. Met Dr Gordon in Max's. Bin outer country, see? Never messed 'bout with you 't all, not this time. Bloody liar! Stop me goin' America. 'right, 'right. Don' care. Don' give a dam'. Only, pretendin' you wash . . . was havin' a baby, when you wasn't . . . Tha's what hurt. Didn't mind not goin' America for baby's shake . . . Didn' mind. But findin' out you bin lyin' even 'bout that . . .'

Sarah was staring wide-eyed, holding on to the far end of the table from him, watching fearfully for the violence she felt sure was to come after he had slopped whisky into his glass and jerked it down his throat, bringing on a paroxysm of coughing which turned his face purple and made him grasp a chair back for support.

'I didn't mean . . .' she pleaded. 'I thought we was making a big mistake. Honest, Tom, I didn't know you'd care so much about . . . You never showed no signs before. I thought all you cared for was money and America . . .'

Her hands flew up defensively as he raised his arm, the one whose hand held the bottle. She ducked her head to one side as he made to throw; but he had not aimed at her. The bottle flew several feet wide of where she stood, to shatter in the fire grate.

'Oh, come on!' she screamed. 'Let's have the bloody lot, then. Glass and all. Come and belt me. Why not get the carvin' knife. Yes! Yes! Take the bloody knife to me. Here . . . I'll get it for you . . . here . . . Aaah!'

Suddenly, as she lurched towards the drawer where the carving things lay, she stopped and staggered, her hands flying to her stomach. She swayed from side to side, and backward and forward, gasping, but without falling.

'Wha' now?' Thomas asked, swaying himself, still holding the glass of whisky he had been about to throw after the bottle. 'Bit more mel'drama?'

'Quick!' she breathed. 'Doctor. Fetch . . . doctor. Any . . . doctor . . . Quick!'

He knew with a chill feeling that this was not an act. There was nothing of acting in the way she was crumpling to the floor, her hands pressing into her stomach. In an instant his flopping limbs were back under semi-control and he was reeling towards the door and almost falling downstairs.

Now it was his turn to look down into a hospital bed. She smiled wanly back.

'Sorry. Tom. I just don't seem able to keep 'em.'

'All right, girl.' He leaned down and kissed her brow.

'No. I don't think I'll ever have one.'

'Ssh! Doctor said you mustn't get depressed. It's all *right.*'

'I mean, I know I told you a lie first off. I didn't want to go to America, that's all. But how was I to know I actually was . . .'

'I told you, it doesn't matter. Only thing is to get you well again. Get you home soon, and I'll look after you myself.'

'Thanks, Tom. How's . . . business?'

'Oh, it's . . . fine . . . fine. Just the same, you know.'

'Really?'

'Honest. Why not?'

They both knew why not. Fresh in Thomas's memory was a visit that very morning from Miss Jenkins, her first since the Bridge House débacle. She came in with a rush, glancing back over her shoulder and quickly shutting the shop door.

'Morning, Miss Jenkins! My word, you look fit to match the sunshine this morning. You're come about those hook and eyes I ordered for you? Well, here they are – by the first post. I'll put them to your account, as usual . . .'

She was fumbling with her purse. 'No thank you, Mr Watkins. I'll . . . I'll pay for them now, and settle what is owing. I . . . I'm afraid I have to cancel my account, you see . . .'

Thomas's mouth tightened. Glancing up, the flustered spinster noticed it.

'I'm so terribly sorry, Mr Watkins. I'd . . . like you to know . . . I do understand . . . a bit. Only, you see, it's not just myself . . .'

He took the proferred money and handed over the little bag of hooks and eyes, with a scribbled receipt for settlement of the account.

'I quite understand, Miss Jenkins,' he said. 'It's been a pleasure doing business with a real lady. Allow me to see you to the door.'

Briefly again they were alone outside the counter. But when he started to open the door she was through it almost before it was far enough ajar to accommodate her.

Thomas turned from the closed door. He caught sight of himself in the long fitting mirror. He moved to stand squarely in front of it, regarding himself from foot to head, with little liking for what he saw.

'All right, Watkins the Haberdashery,' he addressed himself. 'What bloody next, then? Fortune next time round? Eh?'

He returned to the door and turned round the hanging cardboard sign from OPEN to CLOSED. It was a message the ladies of Mortlake would already have decided for themselves.

CHAPTER SEVEN

The business was finished. Thomas knew he would be lucky to get anything near to the price he had paid for the lease, especially if the purchaser happened to hear of the spectacular way in which he had destroyed the goodwill so swiftly built up. A local businessman knew this, too, and promptly made an offer which Tom knew he would be a fool to refuse, even though it meant swallowing a substantial loss. He accepted. The businessman was Mr Bradley-Norton, who turned out to own half the shops in the district already. With great condescension he told Thomas how, under the right manager, the business would quickly pick up again, and his wife's patronage of it would ensure the return of her circle to shop there. For a moment, Tom believe Mr Bradley-Norton was going to offer him the job, knowing he would decline it, but showing off in passing the difference in status between the two of them. But the offer was not made.

'Where to now?' Sarah asked miserably, as she took down her curtains.

Lying in the hospital bed, she had spent much time thinking about the next step. She felt almost certain that he would insist on America this time. She had no way left of fooling him out of it again. She would either have to go, or stay behind and fend for herself. The weakness and depression following the miscarriage were accompanied by a sort of mental numbness. She felt she had no will left to struggle. Whatever life had in store for her would just come along, and she would accept it.

'I've been thinking about that,' he replied, and she waited for the word America. 'I reckon you need a rest to get your strength back.'

Sarah shrugged. 'Fat chance of that. We got to get out of here tomorrow, and no bloomin' where to go, let alone rest.'

'As I said, I've been thinking. If we go over to Paddington in the morning and get a train we could be in Gethyn by nightfall.'

'Gethyn?'

'My home village in Wales, remember? Stay with my Mam. Breathe good Welsh air, eat home-grown food. It'd be the best thing for you, Sar.'

The relief of not hearing America proposed, and of seeing his genuine concern for her, gave Sarah a sudden feeling of elation. She felt that what he had suggested was exactly what she needed: peace and quiet, and a little time of escape from London and its pressures in which to sort out their future.

'You'd like it,' he urged. 'Do you a power of good.'

'Ta, Tom. I reckon it would. Only . . . how d'you know we'd be welcome? I mean, you ain't been in touch with your folks for years, have you?'

'Hardly since Da died. Probably hardly recognise me now.'

'That's what I mean. Can't just turn up again out of the blue, complete with fancy woman, and expect to get taken in with open arms, can you?'

'So far as they know you'll be my wife. They wouldn't have expected me to tell 'em I'd married.'

'Cor, a right close lot you must be. Who is there, besides your ma?'

'My brother Eli, unless he's moved away by now. He's quite a lot older than me. And he's got a wife, Olwen, about half his age.'

'And nippers?'

She didn't notice Thomas's slight hesitation before replying: 'Oh, I expect there's one or two by now. Been married eight years.'

'You seem to know more about them than you expect they'll know about you. What made you leave home, Tom? I've never asked.'

'Ambition. I knew I'd be stuck in the mud if I stayed there. Worked for a lady and gentleman in Llandudno for a time, until they went to Australia. They wanted to make me with them, but I thought London would be the place for me to get on. That's how I came to work for Mr Kirkbridge and then old Bellamy. And met Sarah Moffat.'

'Gawd help us both! The best years of my life, wasted on the likes of you.'

'We've had our moments, Sar. It'll come right again, you'll find. Just want to get you set up properly before we launch into anything new. Give ourselves time to think and plan. Come on – what d'you say?'

'Yes, Tom. I'd like to go to Wales, if you're sure it's all right. Oughtn't you to write and ask first?'

'I think it's better just turning up. Then they can't say no.'

They put their few possessions into a furniture repository, retaining only personal luggage. Next morning, a Sunday, they boarded an early train at Paddington. Sarah slept through most of the journey, lulled by the rhythm of the wheels. As autumnal darkness fell they were in an almost deserted local train entering Gethyn Village station.

No one else got off. The train puffed noisily away. Tom handed their tickets to the sole station hand, who gave him no glance of recognition, and led Sarah out into a cobbled street. It led up a steep slope to a blank-faced little village with a mountain rearing spectacularly beyond. The air was sharp. There was not a soul in sight and few of the terraced houses were showing lights. Nothing seemed to be moving, save slow, curling wisps of chimny smoke, and there was no sound. Sarah shivered.

'I didn't know it'd be like this,' she said, instinctively keeping down her voice.

'Like what?'

'All this . . . Nature. Them hills. No folks about.'

Tom laughed. 'There aren't many folk in Gethyn. Those there are will be in Chapel, Sunday evening. They don't hang about street corners eating winkles here, see?'

As they climbed the stiff incline the sound of an organ reached Sarah's ears. It was playing the introduction to a hymn, and very soon voices joined it. She'd heard a lot about the natural quality of Welsh singing and had wondered whether it was what it was cracked up to be. Her music was that of the halls, all tum-ti-tum and jolly. She was not disappointed by what she now heard, even in this little place. The soaring of the tenors over the growling basses, with a counter-wave of sopranos and altos, sent a thrill through her, standing in the darkness of the empty street, and the great mountain almost lost to sight.

'Mam will be there, and the others,' Tom said. 'Might as well go in.'

He escorted her up to the chapel, which what light remained showed to be an ugly brick building with an unwelcoming aspect. There was a bare porch, lit only by a glimmer through the join of the door. Tom placed their luggage in a corner of it. Her jerked his tie straight and ran his eyes over Sarah. To her surprise, he reached up and undid the string of large coloured beads she was wearing round the neck and put them in his pocket. He jerked his head and pushed open the door. Just as he did so the hymn ended; consequently, the creak of the door sounded loud and prolonged. Every head in the place turned to see who, in Gethyn, could possibly have left it so late to come into Chapel. There were only a few dozen in the congregation, but they packed the small place and gave the impression of being a multitude. Sarah took in at once that every person, man, woman and child, was clad in some sombre colour. She thought Tom needn't have bothered taking off her beads; she stood out enough without them.

The congregation had seated itself and the minister was waiting to begin his sermon. He was a tall man and dark, about Thomas's build, only a good ten years older. His pulpit faced the door through which Thomas and Sarah had come. He was observing them with hard, glittering eyes under bushy black brows, waiting for them to sit down. Tom hastily pulled Sarah into the back pew, where spare hymn books were piled. The minister cleared his throat loudly, to reclaim the attention of those who were still staring round at the newcomers, and gave out his text in a sonorous baritone voice. Sarah couldn't understand it, because it was spoken in Welsh. It was: 'And the Lord said, "Arise and go ye to all the four corners of the Earth . . ." '

'Stone me!' Tom whispered to Sarah from the corner of his mouth. 'My brother Eli!'

Sarah watched and listened with growing fascination. The minister's voice was magnificent, with a stronger lilt than Tom's. As the sermon proceeded it grew louder and his eyes flashed correspondingly. Occasionally he struck the pulpit with his fist for added emphasis, and once even shook the fist at the congregation as he thundered, 'For all those who do *not* heed the Word of the Lord shall fall, and die, and perish in *Hell – for ever more!*' For all that the actual words meant nothing to Sarah, it sounded like no sermon that a chap had sat down and written that morning in his vicarage, but rather a passionate demand, delivered from the depth of his own soul. It was a fearsomely impressive performance, which she would have liked to be able to applaud. It was received with dead silence.

The last hymn was over and the Blessing given. Sarah thought she and Tom would be the first to leave, as they were nearest the door, but he put a restraining hand on her arm, keeping her standing at his side as the minister strode down to take up his position and bid his flock goodnight individually. He gave no sign of recognising Tom. Nor did anyone else, though all stared at Sarah, who got the impression that they didn't much like what they saw. She began to wonder whether they had done the right thing, coming to this unwelcoming hole.

'Here's Mam,' Tom murmured, referring to a wizened little woman, like a bird of dull plumage, who was collecting up hymn books, helped by a young woman of faded, sad aspect. 'And that's Olwen,' he added, 'She's gone off.'

The two women came to deposit the books in the spare pew. Neither recognised Thomas nor made any gesture of welcome to the strangers. They were joined by the minister, now no longer a Thunderer, but the Shepherd. He nodded to Thomas and Sarah, the only person there to have done so.

'Good evening, my friends,' he said in English, obviously taking it for granted that anyone of Sarah's appearance could not possibly be Welsh Chapel.

'Evening, Eli,' reponsed Tom cheerfully. 'Sut yr ydych?'

The little group froze into a tableau before Sarah's eyes: the dominant figure of the minister, black and strong; the tough little bird of a woman, and the other one, limp and careworn; and Tom, cocky and tall, enjoying one of his moments of possession of the initiative.

'Don't say you don't remember me?' he grinned. 'Your own brother Thomas.'

'Thomas?' the clergyman gaped.

'Merciful heaven!' their mother exclaimed.

'Hello, Mam. Hello, Olwen. All keeping well, I hope? Oh, this is my Sarah. From London.'

'I don't believe it,' the minister breathed, referring not to Sarah but to Thomas. His mother proved to be of a more practical turn of mind, though.

'They'll be wanting supper,' she snapped. 'There isn't much.'

'Oh, anything'll do, Mam,' Thomas assured her. The pallid Olwen spoke to her mother-in-law; 'There's an extra bit of stew I put aside.'

Her attempt to be helpful was ignored. '*And* they'll be expecting to stay,' announced Mrs Watkins. 'There's only the attic. Very small.'

'We won't mind,' Sarah said. 'We're used to attics. Anywhere, so long as there's a bed.'

The look she got from Mrs Watkins left her in no doubt that mention of a bed could have only one context, coming from her.

The meal proved to be as frugal as Mrs Watkins had threatened: a minute portion of the stew, a bare spoonful of vegetable, three potatoes each for the two men and two for the women. They all stood for Grace, which Eli intoned in English, as some gesture of respect towards the foreigner,

Sarah. Mrs Watkins showed no such regard for her feelings, however.

'How old are you, girl?'

'I'm twenty- . . . seven.'

'Look older to me.'

'Sarah's been seriously ill, Mam,' Tom explained. He was ignored.

'You have babies?'

'No. 'fraid not.'

'Hm. I trust you help Thomas with his work.'

'Well, course, when it's somethin' I can do.'

'We all can do the Lord's work. Any work, however menial. Even making a bed can be done to the glory of God. I'm going to my bed. Olwen, bring me a hot bottle to my room.'

'Yes, Mam.'

The old lady left without a goodnight, followed by Olwen.

'Well, Eli,' said Tom, putting down the knife and fork for which he could find no more use. 'Fancy you a Reverend! Could've knocked me down with a leek when I saw you standing there in the pulpit.'

'Your face was a bit of a study,' Eli replied, in what Sarah thought a guarded way to a long-lost brother, 'even if I didn't recognise it.'

'I can see Mam's proud of you, Eli.'

'Oh, yes.'

'And Olwen.'

'Er – yes, yes.'

'How long've you bin married?' Sarah asked.

'Eight years come Christmas.'

'No little 'uns?'

'I'm afraid the good Lord has not seen fit to bless our union.'

Their conversation was interrupted by a knocking at the door. Eli looked surprised. 'There's late for callers.'

Sarah had stood up to clear the dishes. 'I'll go,' she volunteered, and went into the narrow hall to open the door to a young woman and a dark-haired small boy. The boy was strikingly handsome. The woman was pretty, too, but there was a strange light in her eyes, giving her an odd expression.

'Nos da,' the woman greeted her.

'Er, I'm English,' Sarah replied.

'Oh – well, I'd like to see the Reverend, please.'

'Come in, then.'

She led the way back into the parlour. It was not the Reverend Eli to whom she addressed herself, though, but his brother.

'Thomas! I saw you in Chapel, but couldn't stop to say hello, because young Melchior here had to get outside quick. So we've come now, special like. Here he is.' She pushed the boy forward. 'Grown, hasn't he? Melchoir, dear, say hello to your daddy.'

CHAPTER EIGHT

The storm had raged on between them in the attic bedroom long after the woman and child had departed and the rest of the family were long asleep. Sarah had got the strong impression that the only one who was genuinely shocked was herself. Eli, and Olwen, who had returned from seeing her mother-in-law to bed, had said scarcely anything. Tom had worked hard at being pleasant to the mother and child, at the same time casting placatory looks at Sarah which had conveyed that he would explain everything later. For that reason she refrained from making a scene there and then. The instant they were alone, though, she turned on him.

'You should've told me, Thomas Watkins. All right, I'm not your flamin' wife, and never likely to be. I got no hold over you. But I've stuck by you, and tried to have your kids, what you couldn't have cared less about; and all this time you've bin smugly thinkin' about this one here.'

He repeated the only words he had been able to get in already: 'Will you listen? That kid *is not* mine.'

'Oh, come off it! All I wonder is that you had the bleedin' nerve to bring me here, knowing they'd be waiting for papa's return. I suppose it's that your skin is so thick you thought you'd get away with it as usual.'

'You calling me a liar?'

'Course I am. It's what you are.'

'Right – that's it! I'm going to the station to sit there all night for the first train back to London.'

'Oh no you're not! You're not runnin' away, my lad. You're stayin' here with me in Gethyn and see this thing out.'

'There's nothing to see out.'

'What – a tart comes to your mother's, dragging a kid and sayin' it's yours, and you say there's nothin' to see out! Either it is yours – in which case you've got me to reckon with – or it isn't; so what the 'ell are you going to do about clearing your name?'

'I . . . Oh, leave it, Sarah. It doesn't matter.'

'Maybe not to you – and your family don't look that bothered – but it does to me. After eight years of my life chucked in with yours, I reckon I'm entitled to an explanation.'

'I've explained. The kid isn't mine.'

'Garn! It's the spittin' image of you.'

'All the same . . .'

'Listen! Answer me this. Were you, or were you not, acquainted with that Bessie Evans eight years ago?'

'Course I was. This is a small village.'

'And you had a tumble with her.'

'No, I did not!'

'But you knew about the kid.'

'Not till a long time after.'

'Oh? How's that, then?'

'I left Gethyn before it was born, see.'

'Very convenient.'

'It had all been planned. I was leaving for that job in Llandudno I told you about. It was arranged.'

'And you just happened to push off from here while she had her bun in the oven?'

'Well, yes. It was nothing to do with me.'

'Bessie seems sure it was. I'd believe her sooner than you.'

'She's a bit touched in the head. Couldn't you see?'

Sarah hesitated. That accounted for the odd look in the woman's eyes. As the momentum of her anger halted, a wave of great misery flooded into take its place. Tears began to splash down her cheeks as she staggered on to the bed, suddenly drained of strength.

'Sorry, love,' Thomas said. 'Just take my word, can't you?'

He moved to put his arm round her, but she jerked angrily away.

Next morning she left him alseep and went down to the kitchen. No one was about except Olwen, who gave her a wan smile and greeting. She seemed to Sarah to mean to be friendly but to lack any sort of spirit. Mrs Watkins was still laid up 'with one of her heads', Olwen explained, and the Reverend Eli was out on parish business: there was to be an extra service that evening, in remembrance of the death of the chapel's founder, forty years ago. She offered to make Sarah some breakfast, but all she would accept was a cup of tea. She felt too dispirited to pursue the subject of last night's upheaval. She said she would go for a walk in the village after drinking the tea.

The grey drabness of the place did nothing at all to cheer her up. The air seemed even colder. The people looked as hard as the stone of their houses and wore the same unwelcoming aspect. The mountain loomed dark and shrouded in leaden grey cloud. London suddenly seemed the most desirable place in the world: she would find no rest cure here.

Only one thing did give her a little excitement when it caught her eye. In a small shop window, so low down that she had to stoop to peer in, she had seen a little flash of colour. Almost unbelievably, it turned out to be what had seemed impossible. It was a tray full of ribbons. Like a stamp collector spotting a Cape Triangular amongst a mixture of cheap rubbish, Sarah recognised the brand as one she had been pursuing in vain on Miss Jenkins's behalf ever since they had taken the Mortlake shop.

'I used to get them from the Robertsons', who were here before you,' the spinster had explained, showing Sarah her only remaining sample. 'Only they ran out of stock, and they were so old-fashioned that it turned out that they had bought what they had about forty years before and the manufacturers have closed down in the meantime. Oh, why can't anyone want to keep such a pretty selection going?'

And here, before Sarah's eyes, was a little mint collection of all the hues, glowing prettily in the greyness of this place. An impulse made her want to possess it. It might even be dirt cheap, scorned as too gaudy by the colourless women of Gethyn. Or it might not be for sale; just for show, something to catch the eye. There was no harm in finding out. If she got some of the ribbons she might even send Miss Jenkins the reel of the gold and the red. They'd been the ones she had really hankered after, and the poor old trout had been more civil to her than anyone else at Mortlake.

She opened the shop door and went in. A bell gave a single loud ping. There was nobody about. Sarah braced herself for the entry of some flint-faced biddy who would tell her sourly that the ribbons weren't for sale. Instead, she heard a scraping, clambering sound. Down a ladder, in a dark corner, came a man's trousered legs and then the rest of him. He reached the floor and turned to her. He was middle-aged, wiry and dry-looking, but with bright though watery eyes. He cocked his head on to one side and smiled.

'Good morning,' he greeted her in English, with an almost comical Welsh accent. 'What may I be getting for you?'

'I came to buy some ribbon,' Sarah answered, nervously for her.

'Ribbon? Oh, I got plenty of that. All colours, all sizes. Red, yellow, green, blue. Nobody wants 'em in this village, except the children, and they're only allowed brown for their pigtails. Might have known better than to stock them, only I liked the colours. Brightens things up a bit.'

'Those . . . in the window,' Sarah suggested hopefully.

'Ah, those! Know a good ribbon when you see it. Ceased making that brand ten or fifteen years ago, they did. Quality. Too expensive to produce nowadays.'

'Are they for sale?'

'Anything here's for sale. Little enough business, without holding stock back. Look round, if you like. All sorts here. Even some pretty garters. The women here would have heart attacks if they saw 'em, but they came in with some bankrupt stock. Help yourself to anything. Original prices on 'em all'

'You don't mean it!'

'If I didn't, I wouldn't say it. No one else is ever going to buy 'em. Besides, I saw you with Tom Watkins in Chapel last night. Old mate of mine, is Tom. Felt quite put out he didn't recognise me. Mebbe I've changed so much. Speaking of which, how about a drop of something, while you're here?'

'Pardon?'

'Look as though you could do with one, you do. Perfect excuse for me, too. Come on into the back room. No hanky panky intended, mind.'

He cocked his head exaggeratedly. Sarah suddenly smiled. His was the first expression of friendliness she had been given in this place.

'All right. Ta.'

'I'll bring the tray of ribbons through, and you can choose what you want. Just through that door. Could just do with a drop of something, this black morning.'

'Mondayitis?' Sarah enquired, as he followed her through into a littered little sitting-room and office.

'Every day's Monday here. Except Sunday, and that's twice as miserable.'

'You bin here long then, Mr . . . ?'

'Jones. Byron Jones. You'll be Mrs Tom, I'm thinking?'

'Yeh. From London.'

'Ah, yes. Never did hear what happened to him. Looks as if he came to no harm, though.'

He gave her a winning smile, screwing the cork out of a partly-full bottle of wine, which looked as if it might be home-brewed. 'Brought you to meet the family, mebbe?'

There was something about the way he asked this, something sharp and sly, that put Sarah on her guard. But he was twinkling his eyes at her in a most knowing way. 'Great deal of difference between Tom and his family, you'll have found.'

'I'll say,' she didn't mind admitting, as she took the glass. 'Cheers!'

'Iechyd da!'

A few moments' silence followed, as they sat there sipping the wine. Sarah turned over the spools of ribbon. 'I like the gold,' she said, as casually as she could, hoping he wouldn't decide to up the price. 'And the red.'

'Tuppence each be all right?'

'Per yard?'

'No, no. The reel. Can't remember what I paid, and can't bother measuring. Wouldn't charge Tom's missus at all, only I got to make a bit to go on buying stuff to make this.' He held up the bottle and poured for her again. 'Seen anyone else, except the family?'

'How d'you mean?'

'Anyone made 'emselves known?'

'Like who?'

'Oh . . .. Bessie Evans, mebbe?'

Sarah knew that he had interpreted her reaction. He explained; 'When I saw Tom come in Chapel with you, I looked over to where she was and saw her watching. Funny eyes, that one, but I reckoned I saw something there. Reckoned she wouldn't be long calling.'

'She did,' Sarah breathed.

'That's why you've got your long face today, then. Where's Tom?'

'Still snortin' in his straw, I 'spect. Right place for 'im.'

Byron Jones sipped his wine, then said, looking into the glass, 'You don't want to believe what you're told, straight off.'

'Who by? Tom?'

'I thought that was the way of it,' he nodded. 'I meant by her. Any of them, except Tom.'

Sarah set her glass down firmly. 'Look, Mr Jones the Shop, or whatever they call you in this rotten place, you hintin' at somethin', then I'd soonest you came out with it.'

'It wasn't Tom, that's all.'

'You know?'

'None better. Well, there'd be one other, of course, unless you count Bessie as two; only, sometimes I don't think she knows any more. Gone further than she looks, she has.' He placed a forefinger to one temple and screwed it round significantly.

Sarah looked hard at him. He was clearly one of those chaps who went to bed drunk each night and only needed another next morning to top him up again. Yet there was nothing reckless about his manner or the way he spoke.

'How do you know?' she asked.

The answer came without hesitation. 'Because on that night . . . the night she says it happened to her, Tom Watkins was never out of my sight. We was poaching.'

'Poaching?'

'Squire's rabbits. Big as sheep, they are. Lovely flesh on 'em. Spent half my life eating Squire's rabbit. Couldn't live off this.' He poured again.

'So Tom was a poacher, too?'

'Not regular, like me. Bit of adventure for him, not serious. Used to ask me to take him out now and then, when he could sneak out of the house. Plenty of dawns we saw together. Including that one. He was with me from dusk to dawn, every minute; and one thing he didn't poach was Bessie Evans.'

Sarah got to her feet. 'Ta very much. You done me a favour, Mr Jones the Shop.'

'Sit down and take another drop. I got nothing else to do.'

'I have, though. Ta, all the same.' She opened her purse. 'Now, for the ribbons – the gold and the red . . .'

'What did I say?' Tuppence the two?'

'*Each*,' she insisted, and handed over the coins. 'You've done me enough favours as it is.' She leaned forward and surprised him with a kiss on the top of his head. And then she remembered to ask him the way to where Bessie Evans lived.

It was a low cottage, at the top end of the steep street, where the village ended and fields began, curving sharply up to become foothills of the mountain. The door was open and Bessie was visible, aproned and doing housework. Melchior was not to be seen. Of course, it was Monday now.

He would be at school. At sight of Sarah advancing Bessie gave a broad, vacant smile.

'Nos da, missus. Nice to have a visitor.'

But Sarah was too angry to pity her in her simplemindedness. She had been working herself up, all the steep way from Byron Jones's shop.

'Right, Bessie,' she answered bluntly. 'I've come to hear the truth.'

'Truth? What truth? Come inside, will you?'

Sarah stepped into the spare interior, smelling of Monday soapsuds; but she had no eyes for her surroundings. She turned round to face the girl.

'You know what I mean. I want to know why you've been blackening my Thomas's name all this time.'

'Blackening?'

'Telling lies about him for years. Making out he's the father of your kid.'

'Oh Duw! I never meant anything wrong. I only told what everybody knows.'

'What everybody *thinks,* don't you mean? I want to know now – who fathered your child?'

'. . . Thomas.'

'It was *not,* and you bloody well know it!'

The girl began to cry.

'And don't come that!' Sarah raged on; 'or I'll shake you till the truth drops out with your teeth.'

'Oh, please, please don't be so angry! I didn't mean to harm Tom. I . . . forget things. Like, who was Melchior's dad. He said God would strike my baby down with some terrible disease . . .'

'Who said that? Never Tom in this world.'

'I forget . . . Said I'd be damned in Hell for evermore . . . And that I would die, too, and suffer the agonies of everlasting Hellfire and Damnation.'

'The – bastard!' Sarah breathed, as something began to dawn on her. 'Don't you see, he threatened that because he knew you was a bit . . . he knew it'd frightened you into shutting up. Yes, and you believed his threats, you poor little cow, and it's made you worse than you was then, I bet.' Sarah's tone changed. 'Listen to me, Bessie. I'm not angry with you, love. You got to do yourself a favour, though, and that's lift all this off your shoulders, where it don't belong. You've got to tell his name, Bessie.'

'I can't! Oh, Duw! I can't!'

'You will,' Sarah told her grimly.

Within an hour she was back in Byron Jones's office. His eyes had lit up when he saw her enter the shop and he led the way into the back without a word. He broached a fresh bottle and refilled their same glasses.

'Found out, did you?' he asked at last.

Sarah nodded. 'I tried bullyin', then cajolin', and it came out in the end. Seems to me anyone could have. I couldn't help feeling sorry for her, but I had to know. It wasn't her fault, I suppose.'

'No more than mine.'

'Yours? What d'you mean?'

'I mean for keeping quiet about it. I knew the truth – only, if I'd spoken out, I'd have been bound to finish up in jug for poaching. Very vindictive man, our Squire. He'd have got Tom jailed, too. But as he was leaving, anyway, it seemed best to keep our mouths shut and let it die down.'

'Hoh, that's typical of men, that is! The poor daft girl's got to live with it for all to see, but the men all cover up each other's tracks.'

'I've often thought that,' Byron Jones sighed. 'Only, it's not quite so bad as you make out. Women – girls – who aren't married expect to get something done to 'em sooner or later, 'specially if they're a bit soft, like Bessie. The other women don't blame them, because they know what it's like. Still a bit primitive in these parts, we are.'

'So much for all your Chapel and burning in Hell, then. Pack of hypocrites, it strikes me.'

'Look, I'll try to explain to you. In villages like this we live a very narrow life. We know most of one another's business, and the only way to hold up any sort of social structure is to turn a blind eye. We got to keep telling ourselves how respectable we are, and behave respectable outwardly . . .'

'And be bloody miserable about it.'

'That's right, 'cept for the likes of me, who keep to myself and know a good cure for misery.' He tapped the bottle's neck significantly. 'I'm as much hypocrite as the rest. Who isn't one, in this world? There's only different degrees.'

'I 'spect you're right,' Sarah agreed. 'Tom's an arch one. I'm one, in my way. I'm not his missus, see.'

She spoke more with defiance than apology. He merely shrugged and returned an understanding little smile.

'Your Toms' not so bad as you think. He's being loyal to his roots in Wales, in Gethyn. He knows that without unquestioning loyalty this community would crumble to dust.'

'Sounds as though it's fit to. It's rotten. And if all you say is what's made Tom change so sudden, the sooner we're back in London, the better. We was gettin' on nice till it all went wrong because of me. And now this . . . !'

She suddenly burst into tears. Byron Jones hesitated, then took the liberty of putting his arm round her and holding her. Her sobs increased. He sat there patiently, holding her for long minutes, refreshing himself from his glass with his free hand, until at length she sat up, to get her handkerchief and blow her nose.

'Sorry,' she mumbled. He made a reassuring sound and gave her the glass.

'Will you take my advice?' he asked. 'Old Jones the Advice.'

'Depends.'

'Don't try to have it out any further with Tom. Let it be.'

'I don't know as I can do that.'

'You know now that he's not the guilty party. Isn't that enough?'

'Yes, but he's the one who's still blamed.'

'So long as you don't need to blame him, it doesn't matter.'

'Look, Mr Jones, you mean very well, and you've been kind, and I'm grateful. I may not be an angel meself, but hypocrisy on this scale makes me want to vomit. All this Chapel, and Bible, and talk of Hellfire Damnation – it's just hollow lies, if everyone's pretendin' about 'em and knows it's all sham!'

'I expect so, to you. It isn't to us who stay on here, because we all accept it. It's our way. You don't belong, lucky for you. Take Tom back to London as soon as you can and forget us on our mountain. Oh Duw! Speaking of Chapel, there's a special service tonight. Just hope I can still stand by then.'

'Why bother? Stay here and open another bottle.'

He shook his head. 'You don't understand. Can't say I blame you, but there it is. I'll be in chapel this evening, if I have to crawl there. And so will you and all the family, because you won't get a train today now, and it'd be too much against Tom's grain not to attend.'

'When I've told him what I've found out, he won't.'

'Please – for his sake – don't. He won't thank you. Don't tell anyone. Just accept it, and go.'

Sarah got up. She swayed slightly. The home-made wine must be potent.

'Feel as if I'll be crawlin', at this rate,' she giggled.

'See you in Chapel,' Byron Jones grinned, giving her a steadying hand to the door. 'Both of us, on all fours!'

She somehow got back to the Watkins home without falling over and stumbled straight up to the attic room. Tom wasn't there. Sarah threw herself on to the bed, just as she was, and knew nothing more until he was shaking her awake. It was very gloomy in the room, but she could see that his expression was one of concern.

' 'ello, love,' she greeted him, and he looked relieved, as if he had been expecting a further row.

'Had a good rest?' he enquired.

Perhaps home-made wine didn't give off fumes on the breath. He sat beside her. 'Yeh – lovely. Where you bin?'

'A long walk. Up on the mountain. Where I always went when I wanted to think a bit.'

'What you bin thinkin'?'

'Oh, this and that, this and that.'

'Tom – can we go home? I mean, to London?'

To her great relief he nodded. 'That was one of the things I thought. We'll get the train tomorrow.'

'Oh, I'd like that. I've had ever such a good rest. Strong air. Good food. I feel like gettin' back now. What time is it?'

'Getting on for five.'

'Five!'

'Olwen says she looked in to see if you were here for dinner, but as you were sound asleep she left you.'

'Didn't hear a blessed thing. Nice girl, Olwen.'

'Yes. Er, look, Sar, there's a special Chapel tonight. Thanksgiving for the founder. You won't mind coming?'

'Do I have to, Tom? I mean, I don't belong – I'm not one of the family.'

'You're supposed to be. It's what we've made 'em believe. It'll be expected.'

'I'd sooner not, love. I've got this headache, see . . .'

'You'll be all right after a good cup of tea. I'll get Olwen to make you one. I'll be going with Mam, so you follow on with her. Right?'

He gave her a quick kiss on the brow and went out. Sarah stayed where she was. She had not been lying when she said her head ached.

It was still throbbing when she and Olwen entered the packed chapel. Again everyone looked at her, and no one smiled, as they entered a pew much further back than the one in which Mrs Watkins and Thomas sat. There was no sign of Byron Jones. A picture flashed through her mind of him making his way there, down the steep dark street, crawling on hands and knees, bottle in one hand, determined not to be late.

The Reverend Eli Watkins entered the pulpit impressively. He announced the special hymn, which was sung with gusto. Everyone seemed to put all they had into it, making a fine combined sound. Sarah mimed, conscious of glances. After what Byron Jones had told her, she was sure their minds were more on the music they were making than on the meaning of the words.

After the 'Amen', Eli prepared to give his address, standing up tall and taking a deep breath, like a soloist about to sing 'Because'. The effect was spoiled, though, by a loud creak from the door and a stumbling sound. Sarah's head went round with everyone else's. Byron Jones stood there – supported himself by the doorpost, rather – leering stupidly. He made a great effort towards the spare pew, almost missed, but made his ground and disappeared with a clatter of hymn books.

Eli, whose expression blended pain and scorn, drew breath again and launched forth.

Once more, he performed thrillingly, doing the founder, the late and long lamented Joseph Ebenezer Elliot-Jenkins as proud as if it had been a cathedral he had founded instead of this ugly little barn of a place. He warmed to his subject and his voice rang louder, as he began to extol their founder's example as a paragon of all the virtues. Sarah risked drawing attention to herself by moving her head slightly, to look at the rapt faces around her. She wondered what lay behind each façade. Had Mr Josiah Ebenezer Elliot-Jenkins really been as good as all that? Must have had a bloomin' miserable life, if so. And all these folks, drinking in their Minister's account of him: how much of it did they really believe, if they even stopped to think about it? When Eli thundered his demands that each and every one of them should go on making their founder's example his own, were they able to believe honestly they'd always had and would?

'Good, upright, steadfast. Faithful in his marriage, ever pure in thought . . . Is it not a pity, nay, an affront to the memory of men as he, that all who worship in this House built by him do not follow his example? And not only in the deed, but in the thought. Whosoever looketh on a woman to lust after her, hath committed adultery with her already in his heart . . .'

Sarah distinctly saw two young men, seated nearby on either side of a girl, turn and catch each other's eye, and turn sharply away again.

'And which of you is free from such thoughts . . .' A spinsterish-looking woman looked most smug at this. '. . . For those who do not purify their thoughts, the Furnace of Fire awaits. There shall be wailing and gnashing of teeth . . .' The congregation cowered almost audibly. 'Yet shall the Righteous be spared, though the Righteous be few. We shall be *very* few! Yet we shall be *spared*, whilst all ye others shall *perish*. "I will heap mischiefs upon thee!" saith the Lord. Evildoers, blasphemers, adulterers, fornicators . . .!'

'What about bloody hypocrites?'

She had not meant to speak out. It had just happened. Something she couldn't resist had forced Sarah's mouth to open and her lips and tongue to form the words, loud and shrill, cutting off Eli's harangue in mid-frenzy. He stared at her, horrorstruck. A great gasp went up.

'Leave my chapel!' he roared.

Sarah stood up, but made no move to quit the pew.

'Hypocrite! Liar! Whited sepulchre!' she accused back.

Thomas, who had turned at the unmistakable sound of her voice, came hurrying back from his pew to clutch her arm and try to drag her out. He had to reach across Olwen, though, and was too much off balance to exert strength. Sarah easily broke free.

'I'm sorry Eli,' he cried. 'She's . . . not well.'

'I'm well enough. And I know all about you, Reverend Eli Watkins. If there's any furnaces of fire waitin', one of 'em's booked in your name.'

'She is possessed of a devil!' Eli cried. 'Take her out.'

Two men rose to obey. Sarah retreated deeper into the pew and flung an arm dramatically towards where Bessie Evans sat white-faced beside her son.

'Go on, Bessie, love. Don't be afraid of 'im. Tell 'em all what you told me.'

But Bessie merely cringed, clutching Melchior to her. Every eye was on her now, including the burning glare of the minister.

'All right,' Sarah shouted. 'I'll tell it, then. That innocent babe, there, what everyone supposed was fathered by Tom Watkins, who's borne the blame for it all these years, wasn't his at all. It was HIS!'

She swung dramatically, to point this time at the pulpit. 'Come on, Eli Watkins. Cast 'ypocrisy aside and admit to 'em it was you had poor Bessie Evans that night in the woods. You're that kid's father, who've bin happy all these years to let Tom take the blame, because he wouldn't come back and deny it for your sake. Tell 'em!'

Several voices from the congregation protested 'No, no! She's mad! She's lying!' But another voice answered them, 'No, she isn't. She's right.'

Every look was turned in a new direction now. At the back of the chapel the head, then shoulders, then trunk of Byron Jones gradually appeared, as he hoisted himself up by the front of the pew.

'All true,' he gasped. 'I can vouch for it.'

'Hold your tongue, Byron Jones!' ordered Eli, who had been silent during the exchanges. 'You're drunk!'

'Drunk I may be. But I know the truth. I was with Tom Watkins every minute of that night. Poaching Squire's land, we was . . .'

'The ramblings of a drunkard and a thief . . . !'

'*And* we saw the Reverend come hurrying out of that wood where Bessie got done. Only, Tom made me promise to say nothing. And because I'm as big a hypocrite as most of us here, I did as he said. Oh, aye, I'm a drunk, and don't mind admitting it. And there's a couple of women not far from this congregation know I've been a bit of something else in my time – though it's they're the adulterers, not me, because I was never married and they were. Don't worry, loves, I shan't tell. It's long over, bless you both. I've had no illusions about what I was. But it took till this morning to realise – to be shown – I was a hypocrite, too. Only one thing I can claim – I was never as deep-dyed a one as *him.*'

He in turn swung round to point towards the pulpit, reeling and falling as he did so. But the object of his condemnation was not there. The black coat of the Reverend Eli Watkins was just disappearing through the side door.

'Why, Tom?' she asked.

'You wouldn't understand, love.'

'I understand more n you know. Me and Jones the Drink had a long and illuminatin' chat. Two of 'em, in fact.'

'Ah, well . . . Did he tell you that here in Wales, the highest honour a family can aspire to is to have a teacher or a minister in the family?'

'Well, no – not exactly.'

'Especially a minister. I knew Eli wanted to be one, at the time I left. Didn't know he'd made it, till we came back the other day. But I was going off to be someone's servant, and he was hoping to serve the Lord. That's why, when Bessie went complaining that one of the Watkins had taken advantage of her, I let 'em think it was me. It didn't matter. I was going, anyway.'

'You bloody daft ha'porth!'

'It's all right saying that, Sar. You don't understand us, that's all.'

'You're not kiddin'! But listen, Tom, do you reckon he'll be all right? I mean, he's bin gone all night.'

'Course he will. He'll be up on the mountain, where I went yesterday. He'll be up there thinking. After a bit he'll square his shoulders, and come down again, and carry on as usual. And they'll still listen to him about Hellfire, and maybe feel a bit more comfortable inside 'emselves because they'll know their minister's earned himself his share like them.'

'Cor! Let's get goin' to that train. I can't wait!'

Olwen came out of the house in the fresh light of the sunny morning. Byron Jones's pony and trap stood waiting to take Thomas and Sarah to the station.

'It's no use, Tom,' Olwen told him. 'Mam won't budge from her room.'

'Ah, well. Hop in, Sar. 'Bye, Olwen.'

He moved to kiss her, but she smiled and climbed in after Sarah.

'I'm coming to see you off.'

There came an angry pounding upon glass from above their heads. They saw Mrs Watkins's beaky face glaring behind a window. She flung it up and leaned out.

'Come out of that trap, Olwen!' she ordered.

'No, Mrs Watkins. I'm going to the station, to see them off.'

'You are not! You'll do as I say, you wicked, disobedient girl!'

'Disobedient, but not wicked. I shan't be long.' As the old woman raved Olwen assured Sarah, 'It will be different from now. I reckon I can handle them both.'

'Good for you, love. Come on, Tom.'

'As for you, Thomas Watkins,' came from above, 'I never want to set eyes on your again.'

Tom shrugged and climbed into the trap after the girls. He pulled the little door shut with a slam. Byron Jones jerked the reins and they went briskly away down the sloping street. None of them glanced back.

CHAPTER NINE

The train taking them to Cardiff, where they would change to the main line to London, rumbled unhurriedly through craggy country. They would be back in the metropolis by nightfall – to what? Life, to brooding Thomas, with the sleeping Sarah's head on his shoulder, seemed just now to resemble an endless game of Snakes and Ladders. Another throw of the dice, a few moves forward to where a lucky ladder signified real progress; then a bloody great snake, to take them slithering back to lose all the gained ground and more.

He had come out of the Welsh fiasco creditably in Sarah's eyes, though she had berated him for a fool for wasting one of his rare noble gestures on that humbug of a brother. And he had to hand it to her for her pluck. The hurt of the trick she had played on him over going to America still rankled; but he could recognise what a mess they'd have been in by now if he had insisted. Fate seemed to have taken a hand there. The question was, what had Fate in mind now? The mind of Thomas Watkins was unusually devoid of inspiration. He had reckoned on two or three weeks in Wales, time to think things out at leisure. But events had hustled them away from there almost before they had arrived. He didn't blame Sarah for that. If he had come clean with her, she might have swallowed her natural indignation and agreed to live alongside the deception until they could get their own affairs sorted out. It had been his mistake not to confide in her, with the result that they were now on their way back to the Smoke with no settled abode and no new enterprise in mind.

Tom's hand went automatically to the packet of bullseyes on his lap. As he groped for one, still staring dully through the window at the moving landscape, he became aware of a little snuffling noise he had been disregarding for the past few minutes. It came from the pretty young girl, who, with a good-looking male companion, were the only other occupants of the Third Class compartment. Tom glanced at them, and saw that she was dabbing her eyes with her handkerchief. The man looked his way just then and gave Tom a sheepish smile.

'Care for a bullseye?' was Tom's fatuous reaction; he held out the bag.

'Oh, er, no thanks,' the man declined politely.

'Would the young lady?'

She nodded. Her grief was evidently not so profound that it could not accommodate a bullseye. 'That's . . . very kind of you.'

She accepted one and popped it into her shapely mouth. Sarah stirred at Tom's side. He had sometimes thought she had a sort of sixth sense where he and other women were concerned. She helped herself to one of the sweets.

'Welsh, is it?' Tom asked the girl, on the strength of her few words.

'It is,' she managed to reply around the obstacle in her mouth. 'Swansea. You, too?'

'Gethyn, near Brecon. Just been visiting the old home. Living in London now. Thomas Watkins – and Sarah.'

'How d'you do?' replied the man, addressing himself to Sarah. Tom noted that his accent was impeccably Upper Class English. 'Grately. Charles Grately. This is Miss Megan Jones, whom I hope to marry.' The girl blew her nose.

'Good for you,' Sarah said warmly. 'Ever such a lot of colds about, isn't there?'

The man and girl exchanged glances. Then he said, 'It's not a cold, actually. Meg's been crying, haven't you, my precious?'

'Anything I can do to help, love?' asked Sarah, with that curiosity which the reading of women's magazines engendered.

'Well . . .' Charles Grately hesitated.

'No problem that can't be solved somehow,' Thomas suggested.

'Dash it, you're right. Do you mind, dear?'

His companion shook her head and managed a little smile. He gave her a hug and leaned across the compartment, elbows on his knees.

'The thing is, we're in a bit of a ticklish situation. You see, Meg and I met last summer, in the park – Hyde Park. She sings in the Doyly Carte chorus at the Savoy, while I, er, guard the King, so to speak, at Buckingham Palace. Coldstream Guards. Ensign.'

'I get you,' Sarah responded with enthusiasm. The combination of handsome Guards officer and pretty chorus girl more than adequately met one of the principal formulae for Romance.

'Marvellous voice,' Grately went on. 'Mezzo-soprano. Great stage presence.'

'Oh, Charlie . . . !'

'No, it's quite true. Had some solo work as well, haven't you, my pet? Anyway, to cut the story short, I'm going to marry her. Just been to Swansea to meet the fond parents. Father's a bookseller. First-rate shop there; everything from learned tomes to penny shockers.'

'But nothin' doing?' prompted Sarah.

'Oh, there aren't any problems there. Only . . . my own parents . . . well, my dear Mama, really . . . Actually, you see, she's the Countess of Andover. I'm Lord Grately, for my sins, but forget about that.'

'I get you. Don't approve of chorus girls.'

'That's it,' the girl chimed in. 'She thinks I just want Charlie for his title and money.'

'Wouldn't be the first to step out of the chorus into a stately home,' Sarah reminded her. 'And your dad a bookseller. That sounds respectable enough.'

'Exactly,' Lord Grately agreed. 'Mind you, it doesn't help Meg's folks refusing to come up to London and meet mine.'

Megan made her accent more pronounced as she

mimicked her father: ' "We're not going all the way to London to be inspected by any earl and countess. Our Meg is good enough for anyone. They must take her as they find her, look you." '

'A true Welshman,' Tom grinned. 'But can't you get your folks to go to Swansea instead, Lord Grately?'

' 'Fraid not. Mama's got it fixed in her head that this is just a little schemer, pretending to love me in order to end up a countess herself and mistress of Grately Park.'

'But I love him for himself,' Megan insisted. 'Truly I do.'

'Have your parents met Miss Jones?' Thomas asked.

'Yes. They even admitted they liked her. But it makes no difference.'

'So if you could convince 'em that it's not the title and money that matter, it would be plain sailing?'

'I think so. The irony of it is that I haven't any money. I shall have some day, of course, but Meg would marry me tomorrow, on my pittance, wouldn't you, precious?'

'Today,' she assured him, and they kissed openly, to Sarah's delight. She glanced at Tom, to share her pleasure with him, and saw that look in his eyes which betokened one of his inspirations.

'What would happen, Lord Grately,' he enquired meaningfully, 'if your parents were to bump into some friends of Miss Jones's family – her godfather and mother, maybe – who were well-to-do, and perhaps English with it, and would give 'em to understand that she had expectations of her own?'

'My dear chap, it might make no end of difference, if only such people existed. They don't, do they, my love?'

Megan shook her head. 'My godfather's got a gas-fitting business in Cardiff. Welsh as they come.'

'So you see . . .' Lord Grately concluded glumly. But Thomas had leaned across the compartment now.

'It could be arranged, though, with just a bit of deception.'

'Eh?'

'That's right,' Sarah chipped in, having recognised

exactly how Tom's mind would have worked. 'You see, Tom and me, we've both had theatrical experience ourselves, which has taken us into very high circles. And funny enough, we once was asked to do almost this same thing before. Lord . . . what was his name, Tom?'

He tapped the side of his nose. 'Promised never to let on, remember? You'd be surprised if you knew, though,' he assured the staring Lord Grately. 'The only difficulty I see is how the meeting could be arranged, casual like.'

'As a matter of fact, that couldn't be easier, perhaps. The parents are up from Hampshire for a few days. It's arranged that I take Meg along with me to dinner with them at the Ritz on Thursday. Do you . . . do you suppose you could manage it then?'

'I don't see why not at all.'

'Well, then . . . No, dash it, it's too far-fetched.'

'You won't say that if it does the trick, my lord.'

'Look, it'd be simpler if you called me Charlie, er . . .?'

'Tom. Tom and Sarah.'

'Charlie and Meg, then. You really think you could do it?'

'Worked last time, didn't it, Tom? Like a dream.'

Thomas said diffidently, 'There would be a bit of expense involved.'

'Oh, Tom!' Sarah protested, but Charlie Grately was nodding agreement.

'Quite realise that. How much?'

'Well, hire of evening dress and jewellery, drinks at the Ritz Hotel, cigar, gratuities, few incidentals . . . Twenty-five pounds?'

Lord Grateley sucked in his breath. 'Bit steep, old boy. Only got my army pay, don't you know?'

'Tell you what, then. Fifteen pounds down, and another ten when it comes off.'

'More than fair. Isn't it, precious one? By the way, what'll you be, just so's I'll be ready?'

'Motor car magnate, from Swansea. Know a lot about motor cars, I do.'

'Good idea. Er, self-made man, perhaps? Wife a bit, er, vulgar?' He shot Sarah an apologetic look. 'But heart of gold, though. Mama's too sharp for you to risk pretending to be gentry.'

Sarah smiled back sweetly. 'We will endeavour to portray the persons you 'ave in mind, Lord Grately. Charlie, I mean.'

'Splendid! Then let's get down to details.'

Thursday evening found Thomas and Sarah at a table in the Ritz. It was in that location outside the restaurant where it was said that one only needed to sit long enough in order to be sure of seeing the cream of society pass by. Frothy pink cocktails were before them and Thomas puffed a fragrant Rosa de Santiago Aristocrato. He wore tails and white tie. Sarah was correspondingly befrocked, bedecked and bejewelled, wearing a wig which gave her some extra years and an appearance of sophistication quite belying her state of nerves.

'Oh, Gawd, here they come!' she fluttered. 'I tell you, we're mad! You shouldn't even have proposed it.'

'Too late now, love. We've taken his money and we got to go through with it. Just keep calm.'

His heart was thudding as much as hers, though, as they watched a party of six, in evening clothes, making its way amongst the tables, towards the restaurant. Megan and an elderly couple – doubtless Lord and Lady Andover – came first, followed by Charles Grately and another couple, middle-aged and of Jewish aspect. Megan was glancing about almost desperately, it seemed. It had been agreed that it would seem more natural for her to recognise her god-parents than for them to accost her. Her eyes at last fell on Thomas and he gave her a quick wink.

'Good gracious!' she cried. 'Uncle Tom and Aunt Sarah. What a lovely surprise!'

Thomas had risen to his feet, Sarah staying grandly seated. 'Well, well!' he exclaimed. 'Little Megan!'

They exchanged kisses with her. Megan said, 'You must

meet my friend, Lord Grately. Charlie, this is Mr and Mrs Watkins.'

Charlie greeted them gravely, then introduced his parents and the other couple, who proved to be a Sir Joseph and Lady Weidler.

'My godfather and godmother,' Megan explained of Thomas and Sarah to Lady Andover.

'Also from Wales?' Lady Andover enquired, pleasantly enough.

'Uncle Tom has a country place near Clydach.'

'Convenient for my factories in Swansea,' Thomas explained.

'Might one ask what sort of factories, Mr Watkins?' said Lord Andover.

'Motor cars.'

'I see. Does one know the make?'

'Not in this country. I hope one day to diversify into the home market, but our present output is entirely spoken for by Germany and Russia.'

'Really?' put in Sir Joseph Weidler. 'You are a private company?'

'Oh yes. Very private.'

'But you'll go public to expand into the home market, of course?'

Seeing that Tom had no idea what this meant, Sarah broke in with, 'I don't think you should detain Meg's friends with a business discussion, Tom dear.'

Sir Joseph made an apologetic bow to her. 'I'm sorry,' he smiled. 'Perhaps another time, though, Mr Watkins? I should be interested to . . .'

The Earl of Andover broke in, addressing Thomas: 'You won't have dined yet, I expect?'

'Well, no . . .'

'Then would you care to join us? I'm sure we'd all be delighted, and I can see Joseph's longing to talk business. He's my financial adviser, by the way, so you can talk as freely as you wish.'

'Well, er . . .' Thomas faltered.

'Oh, do say yes, Uncle Tom,' Megan urged.

Sarah settled it. 'Be delighted, Lord Andover. Most kind.'

'The pleasure is ours, Mrs Watkins,' he responded, with a courtly bow, and offered her his arm.

'Well, now, that's settled,' beamed Lady Andover when they had all ordered, Thomas and Sarah having listened to the others and taken their cue from them. 'How are you managing with servants these days, Mrs Watkins? I'm sure things can't be as difficult in Wales as they are in Hampshire.'

The following two hours passed on this same plane of unreality, so far as Thomas and Sarah were concerned. In for a penny, in for a pound, they played up to it for all they were worth. Besides the seat at Clydach they acquired a London house, whose precise location they were fortunately not asked to state. Thomas's car works were revealed to be turning out vehicles in enormous monthly quantities. An exclusive model had been bought by the Kaiser and the Czar personally and then the jigs and plans destroyed. So far as the main purpose of the operation was concerned, Megan's qualities, as a virtuous and well-connected girl and coming luminary of the international operatic stage, were extolled at every opportunity. Lady Andover was becoming distinctly more interested in her. Lord Andover twice gave Sarah's thigh an absent-minded tweak. Lady Wiedler laughed immensely at what she took to be the native wit of Wales in almost everything Thomas said; while her husband fidgeted, clearly impatient to get down to a hard business discussion with this fortunately-met captain of industry. Charlie and Megan merely had to look coy and throw doting glances at one another from opposite sides of the table.

'I think,' said Lady Andover at last, 'we ladies will take our coffee in the lounge. I'm sure the men want to talk business.'

Everyone rose and she led the ladies away. Sarah went a

little apprehensively, feeling her position weakened by being parted from Thomas. But Lady Andover was insisting that she call her Lettice, so she supposed things were going well enough.

Brandy was ordered and the men clustered together at one end of the table, lighting cigars called for by Sir Joseph Weidler.

'Well, Joe,' Lord Andover asked him, 'how's the Market just now? You know Weidler, Carson, I'm sure, Watkins? Must be the biggest stockbrokers in the City.'

'Oh, of course. How *is* the Market, Sir Joseph?'

'Exceedingly buoyant, just now. This Balkan business, you know. Every other day a fresh rumour of war coming.'

'Blessed if I understand that,' Lord Andover said. 'I'd have thought fears of war would put people off buying.'

'Not in armaments, perhaps,' suggested Thomas, making a bold bid. The stockbroker turned to him, nodding vigorously.

'Absolutely right, Mr Watkins. They're all booming – Vickers, B.S.A., Krupps, Creusots . . . every one. Matter of fact, I'm putting my clients into Vickers Ordinary now. There is a new arms deal with Turkey in the offing. One of their representatives is in Constantinople at this very time. If he comes back with the contract they hope for, Vickers will go through the roof.'

'Really?' said Thomas, his mouth beginning to turn dry. 'I, er, have to admit I'm not well up on Stock Exchange matters personally. I'm really a technical man – a glorified mechanic, you might say. I leave finance to my bankers.'

'Not altogether wise,' Sir Joseph told him. 'Sound, but too cautious. Gilt-edged investment stuff. I'm sure they haven't advised you to get into Vickers.'

'Nothing at all.'

'See what I mean? Take my word for it, when their chappie comes back with that contract – and I'm certain he will before this week's out – anyone who isn't in Vickers will be kicking himself.'

'I hope I'm in,' Lord Andover said.

'Most certainly, Jack. I got you a thousand this morning, on margin.'

'Good for you, Joe.'

'Er, "on margin"?' asked Tom. 'What is that, precisely?'

'City slang,' Lord Andover answered. 'You order the shares at today's price, but you don't fork out the money for 'em until the end of the account. That's a fortnight from tomorrow. In that time, if your shares go up you tell your broker to sell. He takes his cut and sends you the balance, so you pocket a nice profit without needing to put down an actual bean. Do it all the time, don't I, Joe?'

'Sometimes unwisely, I keep warning you. Shares can go down, as well as up,' he explained to Thomas. 'I only advise my wealthiest clients to buy on margin. If things go down before settlement day they can afford to pay up and sit on a loss till the price goes up again.'

Tom moistened his mouth with Brandy. 'Then, if I were to consider buying some Vickers Ordinary on margin, you'd recommend it?'

'Absolutely. You'll need to be quick, though. Could be news from Constantinople at any time, then the price will rocket too high to be worth chasing.'

'You could get them for him, couldn't you?' suggested Charlie, who had watched the performance of Thomas and Sarah throughout the evening with rising admiration for their resource.

'Pleasure. I'd be delighted to open an account for you with my firm, sir,' Sir Joseph told Thomas almost deferentially. 'How many shall we say? Thousand? Two?'.

Thomas swallowed. 'Five hundred. Believe in playing myself in carefully in anything new. Welsh caution, don't you know?'

'Very shrewd, Mr Watkins. I'll do it the moment the Market opens in the morning.'

Lord Andover was getting up. 'That's that, then. And I think it's time we went and made sure those gels of ours aren't getting up to mischief, eh?'

He urged Thomas to lead them from the restaurant, past bowing waiters. As he acknowledged the head waiter's obsequious smirk, Tom suddenly though he knew how Crippen must have felt when they escorted him into the dock at the Old Bailey.

'What a mess!' he exclaimed. It was late that evening. After the dinner party had broken up Charlie had insisted that Sarah and he come with Meg to his rooms in Albany for a nightcap. They were only too glad to accept. Such were their matching natures that a taste of living it up gave them a hunger and thirst for more of it. It would be infinitely pleasanter to linger in full evening fig for another hour or two in those exclusive apartments off Piccadilly than go back to the cheap hotel where they were lodging in Praed Street, Paddington, and discard their hired finery, for return to the shop in the morning. They wanted to keep the illusion intact till the last possible minute.

Sarah had a more practical desire for an immediate discussion between the four of them, though. She explained how Lady Andover had taken such a shine to her that she had insisted how much she and her husband would love to come and dine at the Watkins's town house while they all happened to be in London simultaneously. Lady Weidler, who seemed to have her eye on Tom, had chimed in to say that she and Joseph would adore to come, too. Sarah had found no alternative but to invite them all to dinner on the coming Wednesday. Her only remaining defence was to brush vaguely over the matter of the address by saying that it was 'just near the Park', and promising to send cards to the two ladies.

'What a mess!' Tom repeated. 'You're off your chump!'

'What else could I do? It was you mentioned a town house in the first place. I had to back you up.'

'Yes, but to invite 'em there . . .'

'I tried to get out of it. I said we'd all go to the Ritz again, but they both said they'd sooner come to us. Anyway, you can't talk about landing us in it. What about all them bloomin' shares you've bought? We'll be ruined if you have to pay for 'em.'

'Might make a fortune out.' Thomas sought to convince himself, as well as Sarah. He by no means succeeded.

'What can we do, darling?' Megan asked her swain. 'I feel it's all our fault. It was done for us, and I think Tom and Sarah were marvellous.'

'So do I, my dovekins,' Charlie answered surprisingly cheerfully. 'And I have the perfect solution to the problem.'

'Oh, you're so clever. What is it?'

'Cuckoo Willerby.'

'Beg pardon?' Sarah asked.

'Chap in my regiment. Remember, Meg, I introduced you at the Savoy? Wife Lorna.'

'Oh, I know. Big moustache and a stammer. Always laughing.'

'That's Cuckoo. Well, he's going on leave – safari in East Africa. He's got this whacking house in Hyde Park Square, and he's letting it while he's away. Being Cuckoo, he hasn't done a damn' thing about finding a tenant. Going to leave it to an agent, if he ever gets round to finding one. Well, I'm sure he'd let me use his place for an evening.'

'You don't mean . . . ?'

'Why not? It's fully furnished, kitchen all ready to use, enough dinner things to dine the whole Mess. And, as Sarah brilliantly foresaw, it's just off the Park.'

Hope was suddenly glowing again like a beacon down the vista of Thomas's imagination.

'What about servants?' he asked.

'Ah! Now that's a snag. There aren't any to go with the house. Cuckoo and Lorna are sailing this weekend, so there wouldn't be servants still there on Wednesday. Can't you write to them and get them out of the date, Sarah?'

She shook her head. 'You still haven't won your folks over, and they're going back to Hampshire next Thursday, remember? We got to strike while the old iron's hot.'

'Oh, lor', yes.'

'How many servants could we manage with?' asked Thomas, wearing his calculating look again.

'Well, the least you'd get away with would be someone to cook the dinner, a butler and footman, and say one parlourmaid.'

'What do you think, Sar?' Thomas asked her. 'Rose and Edward might help out for old times' sake.'

'Oh, and Mrs Bridges to cook and Hudson to open the front door – I don't think! You can forget that lot. Better hire some from an agency.'

'That'd cost the earth!'

Charlie suggested, 'I could bring in my soldier servant from Wellington Barracks. Guardsman Cole. He's not a bad cook at all – not that I've had much more than stew from him, out on manoeuvres. Have to keep him out of sight, though. The parents know him.'

'I could help him with the vegetables and things,' Megan enthused. 'I can cook a little.'

'Can you really, darling? I say!'

Sarah said to Thomas, 'What about Tubby at the garage? He's a willing boy. And I know – Dolly Harper, girl I worked with at Barnaby's Music Hall. She's a good sport. She'd be parlourmaid.'

'Still need a butler.'

'Gilbert Brackley! He'd be just right, if old Madg'll let him off the leash for an evening.'

Gilbert Brackley was a burly former detective-sergeant who had been retired from the Force because his drinking habit had come to exceed even that of the general run of detective-sergeants. He had married Madge Fellows, the melancholy widow of the man who had owned the motor business in Kilburn before Thomas acquired it.

'So long as we watch him with the bottles,' Thomas warned. 'Mind you, we'd have to pay 'em all something; and there'd be the cost of the food and drink, and hiring clothes.'

'I'll be responsible for that,' Charlie undertook. 'I'll raise the ante somehow. It all started because of Meg and me, and

I can't think of a better cause to justify a quick grovel to my bank manager.'

'All right, then,' Sarah declared enthusiastically. 'If you'll arrange to get the house and fix the food and things and your Guardsman Whatsit, Tom and me'll do some recruiting. We'd better play safe and have a rehearsal at the house, though.'

'Quite right. I'll telephone Cuckoo about the keys, and we'll try to make it Monday, eh?'

'Top hole, old sport,' Sarah laughed. 'I'm lookin' forward to this.'

'So am I,' said Charlie, pouring final brandies. 'Here's to the Mad Hatter's dinner-party!'

CHAPTER TEN

The costumed cast assembled in the hall of No. 26 Hyde Park Square on the Monday evening. Introductions all round were followed by a speech of semi-explanation from Thomas.

'Right,' he concluded. 'Now, we'll rehearse every single thing that's to happen on Wednesday night, from the moment the front door bell heralds the first guest, up to their final departure. Mr Cole . . .'

'Sah!' responded the strapping Guardsman, who was wearing an apron over his walking out dress.

'You'd better go back down to the kitchen and get used to how everything works.'

'Yassah! Sir?'

'What now?'

'Might I know what you is proposin' to serve – sah?'

'That's a point,' Thomas conceded. 'Any ideas, anyone?'

'Hear you're a dab hand with stew,' Sarah said to the Guardsman.

'You can't serve stew in a place like this!' Thomas protested.

'Why not? What was that we had at the Ritz? Boeuf Bourguignon. Tasted just like glorified stew to me. Make up one of your best, Mr Cole, and chuck in a few handfuls of spices and a dash of garlic. They'll think it's great. Cauliflower and spuds, and some sort of pud.'

'Very good – ma'am!'

Cole wheeled away and through the pass door to the nether regions.

'I'll look out of place as a butler, Tom,' complained Gilbert Brackley, barrel-chested under his starched white shirt front.

'Me collar's a bit tight,' said Dolly Harper, quite a fetching sight in her black and white.

Tubby, self-conscious in livery, merely looked down at the white gloves which mercifully concealed his oil-ingrained hands.

'You'll do fine,' Thomas reassured them. 'Now, we'll run through, if Lord Grately will kindly tell us how the guests will be arriving?'

'Yes. Well, Meg and I will be here already, of course, lending a hand. I'll say we were the first to arrive. I expect they'll come as separate couples, but almost together.'

'Right.' Thomas addressed the three servants. 'For now, I'll ask Lord Grately and Miss Jones to represent Lord and Lady Andover. Sarah and me will be the two other guests, Sir Joseph and Lady Weidler. Got the names, everyone?'

Charlie addressed Megan. 'You've got to be my mama, sweetie, and I'm Father. The butler will be standing by the front door, ready to open it. The footman . . . what's your name again?'

'Tubby, m'lord.'

'That's not a footman's name.'

'How about Albert?' Sarah suggested.

'Very good. You're Albert, remember. And you must be standing here, behind the butler, er . . . ?'

'Brackley, m'lord.'

'I say, what a perfect name for a butler. And the parlourmaid . . .'

'Dolly, sir.'

'Better make it Dorothy, ducks,' Sarah instructed.

'We don't need surnames,' Charlie said. 'Dorothy will be enough. Now you, my dear, must step forward from here and take the ladies' cloaks or wraps, or whatever they're wearing, and sort of spirit them off up to a bedroom. Later on you'll be needed to wait at table.'

Dolly giggled. 'Ever such a good producer. They could do with you down Barnaby's Hall.'

Charlie returned her a charming smile. 'Thanks for the compliment, but let's see how well the show goes, shall we? Right, let's rehearse. Those who are playing the guests will go outside and ring the bell. Got it, everyone? Butler opens door with a polite "Good evening". Guests enter, Parlourmaid takes lady's things, footman takes gentleman's. Butler conducts guests up to the drawing room, asks their names, and announces them.'

'What do I say?' Gilbert Brackley queried. 'What's your name?'

'No, no. Just "Name, please." Very politely and quietly.'

Charlie and Megan, Thomas and Sarah all went out to stand in the porch. After allowing a few moments for the servants to take up their positions, Charlie rang the bell.

Gilbert Brackley opened the door and saw the four of them there.

'Evening, all,' he beamed. 'What was the name?'

After several hours' work they got it as right as they thought they ever would. Cast and principals dispersed, and assembled again early on the Wednesday evening. Thomas and Sarah had been at work in the house all afternoon, dusting and polishing and setting the scene. Guardsman Cole was at work in the kitchen, whistling cheerfully as he stirred the savoury mixture which he tasted frequently and thought not half bad. Megan had chopped potatoes and cauliflower for him and they stood in pans of water, waiting to be cooked. The wine, which Charlie had filched without compunction from Cuckoo Willerby's lavish cellar, was either chilling or taking the air.

Sarah had taken care to hire a different dress from the one she had worn to the Ritz. Thomas had to admit she looked a real stunner in it. He himself was back in tails and white tie, with a scarlet bloom in his lapel. Sarah thought he looked his part to a T and expected to see Lady Weidler giving him the eye again.

'Remember,' she admonished him, 'no buyin' any more bloomin' shares what we can't afford. What happened to them others?'

'Haven't heard a word. I'll ask old Weidler this evening.'

'Oh no, you won't. You keep off business, my lad, or you'll land us in even more trouble.'

'Well, don't you go giving or accepting any daft invitations. All we're here to do is give a good impression for those two kids' sake, then that's our lot.'

'All right then. It's a bargain.'

They both kept it, and the evening proved a considerable success. Nothing grossly untoward happened. Gilbert Brackley announced the Andovers as the Weidlers, and vice versa, throwing the rest of the 'staff' into some brief confusion. Then he tried to announce dinner before there had been time for the first sherry to be drunk, and had to be hissed away by Sarah. Dolly acted her role with expected professionalism, while Tubby positively astonished Tom and Sarah with his polished manner. The food was pronounced excellent.

'Just a little dish we came across in Positano, I think it was,' Sarah answered Lady Weidler. 'Never could remember it's name, so we call it stew.' Much laughter.

Sarah had taken pains to seat Thomas well away from Sir Joseph Weidler, even if it did mean putting him between his wife and Lady Andover. When the due moment came for the ladies to retire she announced that it was a custom she didn't follow.

'Means we either have to miss the jokes, or they have to tell 'em all over again,' she explained. More laughter. What a colourful, extrovert couple! *Nouveaux riches*, of course, but so unspoiled.

To Sarah's relief, Thomas coupled himself with Lady Andover for a stroll round the drawing-room, coffee cups in hands. She herself monopolised Sir Joseph Weidler. He was palpably eager to get at Thomas, but she was determined not to let him.

'Charming house, my dear,' Lady Andover told Tom. 'You must know our friends the Dawnays.'

'I, er, don't think . . .'

'Live next door.'

'Ah, well, you see, we're not often in town. I have to stay in Swansea most of the year.'

They seated themselves on a little sofa, well away from the others.

'Tell me, Mr Watkins, do you really feel that dear little Megan would be suited to Charles?'

'Oh, definitely. No doubt about it.'

'Isn't there? I wonder whether, like you and your charming wife, she would prefer to be her true self in Wales, rather than pretend to this artificial London society life?'

Tom started at this; but her manner was not a challenging one. She noticed his discomfiture.

'I'm so sorry. I put that very badly. What I mean is, it's plain to see that you are happier living to your own rules rather than conforming to society's. I thought it most brave of Sarah to refuse to take the ladies out. I've often felt like it, but I'd never dare. And here you are, in a great waste of a house which doesn't belong to you . . .'

'Oh, but . . .'

'No, I insist. I can sense when a place is someone's home, and their staff are used to them. You've rented this for the season, haven't you? Probably paid a fortune for it, when you'd sooner be comfortable in Wales.'

'Well . . .'

'You see? I knew I was right. I do admire your frankness. So, you really believe that Charlie and Megan are right for each other?'

'Perfect.'

'In that case, you've settled my doubts.'

'Doubts, Lady Andover?'

'Lettice. Naturally, one wonders about one's children, especially where there is the responsibility of a title and estates. One tries to do what is best for them. Of course, dear Charlie will have Grately Hall one of these days. Frankly, though, the family fortune, for what it is worth, is almost all tied up in land and property, so a marriage which will bring some solid cash into the family would be simply ideal. Jack and I like little Megan immensely, but we felt we had to hold back because . . . Well, put in a nutshell, it never occurred to us that she had any such affluent connections as you. And she, the dear, was far too modest to tell us about you.'

'Oh. Ah. Yes, that's Meg all over.'

'I shouldn't like you to think me too prying, but you must see that it would be useful to have some idea of her prospects.'

Thomas answered with great care, 'I'd say that if she married your Charlie, her prospects would be excellent.'

'That wasn't *quite* what I meant. I was referring to her own financial prospects.'

Tom had nothing to lose by answering firmly: 'You must take as you find, Lady Andover. That has been a rule in my life from my mother's knee. Take as you find. With all due respect, that is what Megan is prepared to do with Charlie. He's told her honestly how hard-up he is, with only his pay, and how she can't expect anything more than that for perhaps years to come. She's only too willing to have him on those terms, never mind the sacrifices. I think it our duty to respect their instincts and love, and not set ourselves up to sit in judgment on their decision.'

'Bravo! Oh, I'm sure that speech is so typical of you – the way you do business. Yes, I can see the secret of your success. So you will give the union your blessing, if we give ours?'

'Without hesitation.'

'Then it's settled. It's what I hoped you would say. Jack will be so glad, too. Incidentally, he's taken quite a fancy to your wife, you know.'

Tom could see that from where they were sitting. He switched his charm to full power.

'And I have to you – Lettice.'

The party was over. The guests were gone, including Charlie and Megan, who had had to go with his parents, for form's sake.

Sir Joseph Weidler had been kept away from Thomas, who had been kept away from Lady Weidler. Lord Andover's attempts to persuade Sarah to pop out of the room with him to somewhere quieter had been good-humouredly resisted, though leaving him with piquant hope for a future occasion.

'Well done, everybody. Bloody well done!' Sarah congratulated the wilting, footsore staff. 'Come on upstairs. Have a knees-up and finish off the booze. There's plenty of it left.'

'I could do with a drop,' Gilbert Brackley gasped, tugging loose his stiff collar. 'Quite a strain, that was.'

He had been ordered in advance by Sarah not to go taking sly nips out of people's glasses all evening. It had been a strain for him, indeed, but he had nobly resisted temptation.

'Come on up, Mr Cole,' Sarah bellowed through the pass door into the kitchen. 'Leave the washin' up and come and wet your whistle.'

The Guardsman was up in a flash and they all trooped to the drawing-room. This time the servants served themselves, and their master and mistress likewise. Gilbert worked concentratedly at catching up on lost drinking time and rapidly attained his customary euphoric state. Tubby's remarkable aplomb vanished and he was soon slumped in a chair with an asinine grin on his face. Dolly's drink went at once to her head. She started clamouring for music. A gramophone was found and set going. Sarah partnered Gilbert and Thomas Dolly. Tubby just grinned on.

At length, above the din, the front door bell was heard to give a long peal. Thomas quickly lifted the needle off the record.

'Neighbours.'

'Police.'

'We were making quite a racket.'

'Well, we're here by permission. Straighten yourselves up, and I'll go down and see.'

To Thomas's relief, he opened the door to Charlie and Megan, smiling happily. Megan stepped swiftly forward and gave him a kiss.

'It's all right!' she told him. 'It worked.'

They went up to join the others. 'I say,' Charlie told them all, 'that went off superbly, thank you. My parents said it was the best evening out they'd had for years. Most of their friends are pretty stodgy, don't you know?'

A little cheer went up. Charlie kissed Sarah and wrung Thomas's hand. 'Thanks to you, we've been told we may announce the engagement as soon as we wish. So my gorgeous little Welsh pixie's mine at last.'

Amidst a babble of congratulations and kissing, glasses were quickly recharged and ones provided for the happy couple. Thomas rapped on the table for attention.

'Ladies and gentlemen – on behalf of Mrs Watkins and myself, and our staff, not to mention the employees of Watkins Motor Manufacturers of Swansea, and the staff and tenants at our country seat at Clydach, here's long life and happiness to our young friends, Charlie Grateley and Megan Jones!'

They all drank. The party continued for some little time more, until Guardsman Cole, completely sober on a mixture of five different wines and spirits, announced that he'd have to be getting back to barracks.

'Reckon I'd best be off to Kilburn, too,' Gilbert said. 'Madge'll have words to say, else.'

Since he had one of his customer's cars outside it was arranged that he would ferry Dolly and Tubby also. Thomas went the rounds of each, distributing banknotes from the little wad Charlie had discreetly slipped him. The hired hands went joyously off, leaving Thomas and Sarah, Charlie and Megan.

'Must be going ourselves,' Charlie said. 'You'll stay the night here, won't you?'

'Thanks,' Sarah said, feeling the heavy approach of reality again. 'There's the washin' up and tidyin' to see to in the morning.'

'Don't worry,' Thomas added. 'We'll leave everything as it was. I'll hand the key in at your place, shall I?'

'No rush,' Charlie assured him. 'Cuckoo never got round to finding an agent. I've promised to do it for him, but I'll leave it till the afternoon. Now, come on, my precious. Kiss your fairy godparents night-night.'

Megan did so, warmly, and they turned to the door. Charlie suddenly swung round again, striking his forehead with his palm.

'Dear God, in all the excitement, I forgot!'

'What is it?' asked Sarah, looking round the room.

'Sir Joseph Weidler's message. Says he'd been trying to get to you all evening, Thomas, but somehow never managed it.'

'I made sure of that,' Sarah said emphatically.

'Eh? Well, this message. Vickers got their contract. The ordinary snares shot up to £156. Weidler took the liberty of selling yours out inside the account. He assumed you'd want to take your profit.'

'Oh, yeh. Yeh. If there's no money to be found.'

Charlie laughed. 'Certainly not by you. You've made a killing, don't you know?'

'How . . . how much?' Sarah asked and held her breath.

'Near as dammit, two thousand.'

'Two . . . thousand . . . pounds?'

'In round figures.'

He and Megan watched from the doorway, delighted at the surprise and joy he had been able to give these two people who had done them such a good turn. Sarah turned to them, wide-eyed.

'How . . . much would your friend be wantin' to rent this place by the week?'

'Can't say offhand. Up to the agent, really.'

'When you see him, will you be so good as to tell him to give us first chance? We'll wait here to hear from him in the afternoon.'

'With the greatest of pleasure, my dear. Now, must dash. Toodle-pip!'

The young couple went. Sarah groped for a full glass and sank into a chair. Thomas did the same.

'We're alseep, aren't we?' he said. 'Dreaming it.'

'I just pinched meself, and if we are, it didn't wake me up.'

'Then it's got to be true.'

'Yeh. Said the right thing, did I? About renting this?' They stared around the room, fine despite the party litter. 'I mean, it'd be nice to live in luxury for a week or two. Wouldn't need no servants. Reckon we could afford it?'

'I tell you what I reckon,' Tom answered. 'Three months, he's gone for, isn't it? Then that's how long we take it for. *And* get some servants. Time we had a decent place of our own, Sar.'

'Yeh,' she said. 'Reckon we've earned it – you and me.'

CHAPTER ELEVEN

The arrangement was easily made. The agent came hurrying round early next afternoon, awaited tensely by Thomas and Sarah. He told them that, from previous experience of letting for Mr Willerby, he would only be concerned to have someone in residence who would keep the place up. The rental would be quite nominal, therefore, and anyone recommended by Lord Grately, as they had been, would be acceptable without question. So Thomas was able to take a taxicab over to Paddington and settle up for their room there. He soon brought back with him their few belongings, to find Sarah aproned and drying dishes.

'I finished tidying upstairs,' she told him. 'Just these, then we're back to normal. 'Least, as normal as it's goin' to seem.'

'You'll get used to it. And the sooner we can get some servants in, the better.'

'I'm not too sure about servants, Tom.'

'Why ever not? Don't go thinking we can't afford 'em.'

'Well, that does worry me a bit. I can manage the place. There's only two two of us to cook for, and that.'

'I told you, we're going to live in style. We've earned it.'

'Yeh, but servants . . . It's not *us*, is it?'

'We'll treat 'em all right. Open their eyes a bit when they find their employers mean to be friends.'

Her qualms left her at once. 'That's clever! Treat 'em better than we ever was. Then invite old Hudson round and give him an eye-opener how to keep a happy staff.'

Thomas grinned and gave her a happy hug. 'And a happy master and mistress. We're going to live it up, my girl. So just you get rid of that towel and get out to Knightsbridge for some clothes.'

'I'm all right.'

'Sarah!'

'Oh . . . right, then. 'Spect you'll be off to Saville Row, knowin' you.'

'How did you guess?'

When they met again in the early evening they were both transformed, Thomas had bought a smart suit off the peg, to be going on with, and a hat, gloves and cane. He sported a buttonhole. Sarah was looking equally fine in a serge skirt, frilly blouse and jacket, moulded perfectly to her figure. She was accompanied by a uniformed delivery boy, carrying a bag of provisions and a parcel containing the clothes in which she had gone out. Tom gave him threepence.

'Harrods,' she said, when the door was closed. 'Like it?'

'Smashing.' He struck an attitude, showing off his own rig.

'Oh, very sharp! Thought you'd be having your suits made, though.'

'I ordered two, but they'll take a while. This'll do for now.'

'Yeh. I ordered three frocks. How much the suits cost?'

'Dunno. They didn't want paying.'

'No more did Harrods. The minute I said I was Mrs Watkins of 26 Hyde Park Square their eyes went all misty. D'you know, apart from the cabs, I haven't spent a bloomin' ha'penny.'

'Same here. They say the King never has money in his pocket.'

'There'll be bills one day, mind.'

'And more money to pay 'em with. Old Joe Weidler was on the telephone just before you came in. Asked if he could put some of the money into Jarvis Textiles. Reckons they'll be half as much again this time next week.'

'Tom,' said Sarah anxiously, 'you won't risk our cash, will you? I mean, even Weidler can't always be right.'

'Don't you worry. Anyway, I'm buying on margin again. Get another profit with no need to pay out.'

'It's like Harrods, isn't it? Walk out of there with all this on me, and nothin' to pay. Take some gettin' used to.'

'We used to live in old Irvine's flat without paying, didn't we?'

'Only 'cos we couldn't. He was always after his money, when we hadn't any. But now we got plenty, they don't want it. Funny old world.'

'Isn't it? Anyway, let's make a nice cup of tea and talk about the servants. I've been making a list.'

Next morning Sarah telephoned Mrs Hunt's renowned domestic employment agency in Kensington, insisting on speaking to that lady in person. She told her that she was setting up a new establishment in Hyde Park Square and would be prepared to consider an experienced butler, cook and parlourmaid. By late morning the second of these stood before her in the drawing-room.

'Sit down, won't you?' Sarah smiled. 'I'll just take a glance at the references. Nice day, for the time of year.'

'Madame.'

'Mm. Speaks highly of you, Mrs Ambrose. How fancy is medium-fancy cooking? My husband will be entertaining business gentlemen.'

'They're the easiest sort,' answered the middle-aged woman, who had the rather ferocious air of most cooks Sarah had known. 'Saddle of mutton or rib of beef's all they ever want. I do galantines and ice bombs.'

'That sounds satisfactory.'

'And cucumber soup and salmon tart. And I keep a stock pot, so there's always a beef-tea for eleven o'clock.'

'That sounds nice, dear,' Sarah approved, her mode of address causing Mrs Ambrose to bristle visibly. 'We don't intend to be a very grand household.'

'I hope there'll be a kitchen girl, madam.'

'A kitchen girl? I wasn't thinking . . .'

'I couldn't come if there isn't one. I doubt if any of Mrs Hunt's cooks would.'

'Oh, I see. Well, in that case . . . Yes, there will be.'

'Then that's quite satisfactory, madam.'

Also in the drawing-room, a few hours later, Thomas

faced a not dissimilar situation. He was interviewing a lofty butler named Wilson.

'Take a seat, Mr . . . er, Wilson.'

'Thank you, sir, but no. Might I enquire whether you are from abroad, sir?'

'No. Why?.

'The idea of a butler sitting down, sir. Forgive the observation, sir.'

'Look, we're not pretending to be out of the toppest top drawer, you know. We want this household to be comfortable and happy, for all of us – the servants included.'

'*Happy*, sir?'

'That's it.'

'None of Lord Pinner's staff was ever happy, sir – God rest his lordship's soul.'

'Exactly. And you hated him.'

'Certainly not, sir. Even the lowest of the low – and in my opinion sir, that is the valet – even he knew that a kick from the master was for his benefit. Speaking of valets, sir, I trust there is a footman to double?'

'I don't want a valet, and we don't need a footman. I've a feeling you'd be a bit too grand for us, Mr Wilson.'

'Wilson will suffice, sir. As to bein' grand, sir, I don't think you'll find any butler worthy of the name who will work without a footman. And might I enquire, sir, whether we have appointed a cook and parlourmaid as yet?'

'My wife's seen the cook,' Thomas answered unhappily. 'She's seeing a parlourmaid and kitchen girl this afternoon.'

'In that case, sir, we shall only require a footman to complete our household. And now, perhaps I might look at the quarters, sir?'

'It's warm in here,' Thomas complained, entering the drawing-room in the evening of the day following. He began to peel off the jacket of his day suit.

'No, Tom!' Sarah warned. 'It wouldn't be proper.'

'I'm not sure it's proper for 'em to light a fire we didn't ask for.'

'You know it's the rule. Fires whether you want 'em or not, till the end of March. After that you freeze to bleedin' death.'

'We shan't freeze in this house. We shan't stifle, either. If I want to take my coat off, I . . .'

He broke off, jacket half-dragged from one shoulder, as Ethel, the nice-looking parlourmaid, entered. She curtseyed. 'May I see to the curtains, madam?'

'Help yourself, love.'

The girl wordlessly attended to drawing the curtains, curtseyed again, and went out. Tom had struggled guiltily back into his jacket at her entry. He hesitated whether to start taking it off again. There came a tap at the door, and John, the young footman, came in.

'See to the fire, sir,' he explained.

They watched impatiently while he fiddled with poker and tongs, placing single pieces of coal strategically. Then he left, with a little bow.

'Like Piccadilly Circus,' Thomas growled.

'It's the way. Never thought of it like that when we was in service. Had a good day?'

'I went to Weidler's office. Those textiles jumped, like he said, so we took our profit. That's about all.'

'Not much to show for a day. Suppose we'll get used to it. Fancy a drink?'

'I could go a brown ale.'

'You'll be lucky if there's a drop of brown ale in all Hyde Park Square. Ring the bell and find out.'

'It doesn't matter . . . You ring, if there's something you want.'

'They'll all be busy over dinner . . . Don't even know if the bell works.'

'Course it works!' Sarah jumped up and went impatiently to pull the brass knob. But she almost scurried back to her seat. She was just in time for Wilson to appear.

'You rang, sir?'

'I? . . . Oh, yes. I, er, thought there might be time for a whisky and soda before dinner.'

'Yes, sir. There is time before you change, sir. I have the tray outside.'

He went out and returned immediately, carrying the tray with decanters, glasses and syphon. He began to prepare Thomas's drink.

'I'm not changing,' Tom said.

'Not changing, sir?'

'Only the two of us. We'll be informal tonight.'

'Informal, sir?'

'*We will eat as we are.*'

'In the dining-room, sir – or here, off *trays*?'

Sarah snapped, 'In the dining-room, as we are. And I'll have a port and lemonade now.'

Wilson raised his nose from placing Thomas's whisky before him. 'I regret I did not think of bringing port wine *before* dinner, madam. I will go and fetch . . .'

'Oh, save your feet. Got some *sherry* wine there?'

'Indeed, madam.'

'A noggin of that'll do.'

The butler poured, seeming to suffer some pain as he did so. He placed the glass on a table near Sarah, together with a small plate of biscuits, then departed agonisedly.

'I didn't ask for bleedin' biscuits! Spoil me dinner.'

'He knows best. Eat 'em.'

The calling cards began to be left, bearing other addresses in Hyde Park Square.

'What am I supposed to do about 'em?' Sarah asked Thomas, who knew more about such things than she.

'Drop your own card back. Ask 'em to tea.'

'I haven't got a bloomin' card.'

'Telephone 'em, then. Write a note.'

'You write for me, love. Your hand's ever so much better than mine.'

'All right. Who are they, anyway?' He picked out 'Who's Who' from the revolving bookcase.

'Number twenty-two. Lady Hillingdon. 'Ere, she's next door but one. Wonder if she's had her eye on us?'

'Most likely. "Hillingdon, Lord . . . Partner in Cohen, Hull and Hillingdon, merchant bankers." Could be useful. Who's the other?'

'Mrs Sankey. Number thirty-seven. That's the other side. I think they consider it the snob side.'

'Well, they're wrong, 'cos they aren't in here. I'll write to 'em both after dinner.'

The invitation for next afternoon were promptly accepted by the two ladies. Sarah received them grandly in the drawing-room, with tea things at the ready. Ethel, whom she liked as being a willing, approachable girl, helped her serve. Both ladies were middle-aged and utterly self-assured.

'And what does your husband do, Mrs Sankey?' Sarah enquired.

'He's a solicitor. And yours, Mrs Watkins?'

'He makes motor cars. Has a great factory in Wales.'

'Curious,' remarked Lady Hillingdon. 'I believe this is the first time we have had Trade in the Square, Mrs Sankey?'

'He's in the City, too,' Sarah amended hastily. 'That's where he makes most of his money.'

'Surely my husband must know him then. He knows everyone in the City.'

'If he knows Joe Weidler, then he'll know Thomas Watkins.'

'Ah, Sir Joseph. Of course.'

'That will do, thank you, Ethel,' said Sarah, with a secret wink. 'Mrs Ambrose will have plenty for you to do, with eighteen coming to dinner.'

'Oh, yes, madam. There's all the best silver to see to.' The girl gave them bob and went. Sarah resolved to do her a good turn sometime.

Talk was desultory throughout tea, largely consisting of Lady Hillingdon and Mrs Sankey scoring points off one another as to the merits of their respective houses. When Sarah could stick no more of it she said brashly, 'I do hate small talk.' The ladies stared at her. 'I mean, being a woman is so boring anyway. You can get small talk in shops. Look, have another cup of tea and some of Mrs Ambrose's special cake – it's got six eggs in it – and let's have a cosy chat?'

'Upon what subject?'

'Anything women aren't supposed to discuss.'

'Oh,' said Mrs Sankey, blushing, 'nothing naughty, I hope. I can't carry on a naughty conversation. I blush, you know.'

'I didn't mean that. I meant anything else that men think belongs to them alone. Such as money.'

'Money?'

'F'r instance, I take an active interest in the share market, myself.'

'Oh, but so do I,' Lady Hillingdon replied promptly. 'Between these walls, I pick up a good deal more from my husband's conversation with his friends than he thinks. I have my own account with another broker, in my maiden name.'

Mrs Sankey, blushing even more hotly, confessed, 'So have I.'

'You don't! And to think that all these years we have been neighbours . . .'

'You see,' Sarah crowed. 'If I hadn't suggested a proper chin-wag you'd never have found out. Do have some more cake. Shall I ring for more tea?'

'That *would* be nice,' Lady Hillingdon said. 'But tell me, Mrs Watkins, are you in tin?'

'I don't think so.'

'Good. Because it's about to collapse.' She leaned towards the others, lowering her voice. 'My husband overheard a certain conversation in his club yesterday . . .'

The threatened demise of the tin industry having been dealt with, they turned their attention to shipping. Mrs Sankey asked, 'Has either of you any views on Harbottle Shipbuilders?'

Lady Hillingdon threw up her hands. 'No one in this Square could be so unfortunate as to be in Harbottle's.'

'I am,' Mrs Sankey blushed.

'Great heavens! My dear, you must know at once that Enoch Harbottle, without whom the company is nothing, is at death's door. Quite beyond hope of recovery. In Newcastle Cottage Hospital. Under an assumed name, of course.'

'Oh, my goodness! What time is it? Oh – 'Change will be shut for today.'

'You must pray he lasts the night, and instruct your broker to sell out first thing in the morning. In fact, if you'll accept a further word of advice, tell him to use the funds to buy at once into Bella Second.'

'What do they make?' asked Sarah.

'Bella Second is a gold mine.'

'So is Jarvis Textiles. We bought at two-and-six, and they're four shillings now.'

'No, no, my dear Mrs Watkins, you misunderstand. A gold *mine*. The newest and deepest in South Africa. This is strictly between ourselves, but the quality of the ore has been known for months and they are about to go secretly into production.'

Mrs Sankey said in a thrilled voice, 'So we can still buy?'

'For only tenpence. When the news comes out they will shoot up into pounds.'

'In that case,' Sarah mused aloud, 'it sounds like a switch from Jarvis Textiles.'

'The sooner, the better. But I beg you – both of you – not a word!'

But Sarah told Thomas, of course. He looked sceptical. 'Reckon I'll give Joe Weidler a ring about it first.'

'No, Tom! He'll start putting everyone else in – Lord Andover, all of 'em. The price'll go whizzin' up. We got to get in first.'

'You've only got Lady Hillingdon's word for it. How do we know she knows what she's talking about? I never heard of women playing the Market. Don't seem right.'

'No, it wouldn't to you, because you're a man.' Sarah rubbed her nose suddenly and violently with the back of her hand. 'There you are! The nose-itch. Remember that time it itched, and I told you what to back in the Derby, and it won at twenty-to-one, only you hadn't put the money on?'

'Well . . .'

'It'll be pounds for pennies for sure, Tom. You'll see.'

This time he did as she advised, contrary to the counsel of Sir Joseph Weidler, who, when Tom telephoned to order the transaction, assured him he was making a grave error. Tom swallowed, and insisted. Within a week the news of Bella Second came streaking through the City. The shares went to forty-five shillings.

'What'd I tell you?' Sarah triumphed. 'Pounds for pennies. Now it's a gold mine both ways.'

CHAPTER TWELVE

Doubtless it was through Sir Joseph Weidler, who scrambled into the Bella Second shares soon after they began their spectacular move, that the name of Thomas Watkins became associated with the tip-off. One or two of Sir Joseph's clients to whom he mentioned this remarked that they would like to meet his new source of inside information. When he told Thomas, the latter responded with the ready gesture of inviting them all to dinner. It was to be an all male affair, and he did the additional decent thing by inviting Lord Hillingdon and Mr Sankey as well.

The carriages were expected shortly. John, the footman-valet, was helping Thomas with his shirt studs.

'D'you have any ambition, John?' he enquired expansively.

'Me sir? Breathe in, sir, please, Oh, yes.'

'Not to go on waiting on people, I hope.'

'That's right, sir. One day I hope to be a butler.'

'That's all?'

'All, sir? What more could there be? I do get depressed about it, though.'

'All right, leave the rest of 'em to me. Just pass my tie, will you? Why depressed?'

'When I look at Mr Wilson, sir. I could never be as good as him. When I watch him, I know I'll never be more than under-butler at the most, and probably not in a best house at that. Your tie, sir. I ironed it for you.'

'Even though it's new? Bet you didn't iron my bootlaces.'

'No, sir. Should I have?'

'I've heard of it, in what you call "best houses". What do you call this one? Second-best?'

'This is Hyde Park Square, sir,' was the flustered young man's ambiguous answer. Tom grinned at him. 'Not quite Eaton Place, though.'

'Sir?'

'Never mind. That's all, thanks.'

Sarah had entered. She was wearing a peignoir, slippers, and, incongruously, pearls. Her expression was discontented.

'Better cover yourself up a bit,' he said, nodding towards her half-exposed bosom. 'Be giving that boy ideas. What are you slopping round like that for?'

'It's a men's dinner. Nothin' for me to dress up for.'

'Why the pearls, then?'

'Best for 'em, next to the skin. Anyway, why shouldn't I dress how I bloomin' like? No one's coming to see *me*.'

She had protested from the first about this notion of a gentlemen's dinner. 'Just want to get away from your wives, I suppose. Men!'

'To talk business. No chatter.'

'It's daft. Who was it put you up to Bella Second? Me! Who tipped you off? Lady Hillingdon, not bloomin' Lord. Why shouldn't we be in one the business talk?'

'Listen, Sar, we've been lucky twice – three times, if you count Jarvis Textiles – through other people's tips. These lot are experts. They know what they're talking about. I've got a lot to learn from them.'

'You'll learn more from me and their wives, if you'll listen.'

They heard John's tap at the door. 'Excuse me, sir,' he said. 'The first carriage is arriving.'

Sarah gave Thomas a relenting kiss. 'Go on, love. Have a nice time.'

He went off and she stayed in the bedroom, staring at herself in the dressing-table mirror, feeling like some unheeded spare part.

She was still there an hour later, lying on the bed, when Ethel came in, bearing a tray with covered dishes and a half-bottle of wine.

'Sorry it's been so long, madam, but it's hectic down there. The gentlemen are really going at it. While the soup was coming out, the beef was going in, and we could hardly draw breath.'

'Put it down anywhere. I'm not all that hungry. It's a lousy idea, a men's dinner.'

'My former gentleman was in business, and he had them all the time.'

'Huh. I bet I know better rude stories than they do.'

'Please eat it while it's hot, madam.'

'Oh, all right. Stay and have a chat with me.'

'I daren't, m'm. Quite apart from all there is to do, Mr Wilson wouldn't allow it.'

'I see. It's his house, then?'

Ethel fidgeted, searching for something to say that might appease her pouting mistress. All she could think of was : 'Sometimes they have an entertainment.'

'Who does?'

'The gentlemen – at their dinners. Usually something refined. Once – oh my word! – the chief guest was the Governor of the Bank of England. They lashed out that night. Got Madame Patti to sing. But I dare say you and Mr Watkins didn't like the idea of an entertainment.'

'No,' Sarah replied, thinking. 'We don't like to be flash, you see.'

The men were drifting back into the drawing-room, rumbling discreetly and smoothing creased coat tails and trousers after two hours' sitting. Wilson dispensed cognac and cigars.

'Excellent dinner, thank you,' said one of the guests to Thomas. He was plump and sleek from habitual good feeding, and the others had tended to listen keenly when he spoke. Sir Joseph Weidler had brought him, having told Tom quitely in advance that this was Henry Tanby, a millionaire several times over on the strength of a diversity of business interests.

'Been looking forward to having a word with you,' he went on. 'You strike me as a young fellow to watch. Bit of a pioneering type, I fancy. I have the feeling motor cars are here to stay.'

'I know they are.'

'That's why most of these others are here tonight, no doubt. Think they see a painless way of getting in. Assume because you're young you won't be so astute as Willy Morris or Herbert Austin. Oh, blast!'

His displeasure was at being interrupted by the arrival at their side of Lord Hillingdon and Sir Joseph Weidler.

'Want a talk with you, Watkins,' Lord Hillingdon said.

'I'm having one,' said Tanby. Lord Hillingdon, though, was not one who deferred to this particular millionaire.

'When's this motor car business of yours going public, Watkins?' he persisted.

'Leave that to me,' interrupted Weidler smoothly. 'I'm his broker.'

'Take more than you to launch it, Joe. He'll need my bank. Now, Watkins, when am I going to see your figures?'

'Ah . . . yes . . .' was all Thomas could manage. This was a moment he had anticipated ever since that particular deception had been impetuously launched. He had often tried to envisage how he would get over it, but had found no clear solution.

'Suppose you've seen then,' Lord Hillingdon remarked to Weidler. Surprisingly to Thomas, the latter had never raised the question. Now, he merely tapped the side of his nose and looked inscrutable.

'Well,' the other said, 'the market's very buoyant just now. Don't delay too long.' He gave Thomas a searching look. 'You *are* big enough to go public, aren't you?'

'Of course he is,' Sir Joseph intervened. 'How many cars a week is it, old man?'

Thomas replied airily. 'Varies a good deal, you know. More in summer.'

To his relief Henry Tanby took over the conversation again.

'I gather you're well into Bella Second.'

'I bought at tenpence.'

'Well done!' Lord Hillingdon exclaimed. 'So did I. Thought I'd beaten everyone to it.'

'Have to get up early to beat Thomas,' Sir Joseph Weidler told him, and the two drifted away.

'Very smart of you,' said Tanby. 'They were up to twenty-six when I bought. Still, I shall have doubled by the end of the week, so I'm satisfied.' He glanced round swiftly, then went on, in a lower tone. 'About this motor car company. In Wales, I believe?'

'That's right,' said Thomas, wary again.

'You going to let those vultures see your figures?'

'I haven't committed myself to anything yet, Mr Tanby.'

'If you want to do yourself a favour, you'll show 'em to me first.'

'Well . . .'

'Tell you the truth, only one thing puzzles me. I can't find a trace of it in any register.'

'Ah . . . well . . . It's a private company, you see.'

'Yes, but not a *trace*.'

'Really?'

'Most odd. In fact, we couldn't find a single motor car manufacturer in the whole of Wales. Not one. There's a chap who has a bicycle factory near Swansea; but no cars.'

Thomas put on what he could only hope was a mysterious look.

'I have my reasons for that,' he said.

'No doubt, no doubt. It just occurred to me, though, that if you'd be prepared to give me a modicum of information – round figures would do – it might well enable us to talk further, to our mutual advantage.'

Cornered, Tom was beginning to mutter something indecisive about having special reasons of his own for preferring not to go into details for the moment, when a sudden intervention saved him. It was the entry of Sarah. She was a dazzling figure, in a silver dress with many clusters of sequins. Jewels twinkled at her throat and gloved wrists, and tall white plumes bobbed over her upswept hair. The guests regarded her with anything but hostility.

'Gentlemen,' she announced dramatically. 'I am devastated to have to tell you that your evening is ruined.'

The first thought of every one of them was that there had been a Stock Market crash; but that, of course, was impossible at this hour.

'My planned surprise for you is not to be.'

'Surprise?' Tom breathed to himself suspiciously. She'd been in that resentful mood earlier on. Maybe she'd drunk herself out of it, or else she'd cooked up some idea of wrecking the evening to get her own back for being kept out.

'The entertainment,' she continued. 'Madam Clara Butt was coming to sing for you. She has sent word that she has the most dreadful cold and can hardly speak, let alone sing.'

Bloody little liar! thought Thomas admiringly. It had certainly produced an effect: Clara Butt was at the peak of her fame, a household name. But Sarah was going on.

'I hardly like to suggest it, but I thought, rather than you have no entertainment at all, I'd offer to sing for you myself. I was professionally trained, wasn't I, Thomas?'

'Oh . . . yes, yes.'

There were murmurs of approval.

'Mind you, I'm no Clara Butt.'

The men all laughed. It was Henry Tanby who spoke out for them.

'Mrs Watkins, what you may lack of Madam Butt's fame as a singer, you more than make up for in decorativeness.'

'Here, here!'

'If you would do us the honour to sing, I'm sure we should all feel privileged.'

Sarah went to the piano and selected a piece of sheet music from within the stool. The men assumed deferential listening postures. Just typical of her, Tom thought. No keeping her out of anything.

Her piano playing was rudimentary, but adequate for the ballad, 'I dreamt that I dwelt in marble halls', which she sang in a small, clear voice which was strange to Tom, who had only heard her bellow music-hall ditties. From the glances the others were shooting one another, and the raised eyebrows, this was clearly not the way they would have chosen to pass the time. She was good to look at, but that was all. Tom began to cringe inwardly, imagining his guests already thinking up excuses to leave.

Not for the first time, though, he had underestimated Sarah. She could sense the restlessness, too. She had expected it, but had had to adopt these tactics. It would have been too blatant to launch bluntly into what she had in mind. But now was the time. Instead of beginning the third verse, she suddenly altered the style of her playing to the unsubtle vamping style of the public-house pianist. The gentle ballad she had been piping gave way to a raucous ditty familiar to galleryites throughout the land, accustomed to nudge one another at each double-meaning and to roar out the silly, rumty-tumty choruses.

The expressions of polite boredom around the drawing-room were transformed to ones of astonishment, then incredulity, then delight. With one accord the company unfroze from its tableau of gentility to crowd around piano and performer, glasses and cigars waving in time to the tune. When the chorus came there was not one who didn't join in.

'Splendid!' cried Sir Joseph Weidler over the pandemonium of congratulation when it ended.

'Remarkable woman,' Lord Hillingdon told Thomas. 'Makes one begin to wonder what our wives get up to when they're alone.'

Tom could relax at last. If only you knew, he smiled to himself.

'Didn't do no harm, did I?' Sarah demanded, when the guests had at last gone. 'Helped to make it go.'

'Clara Butt indeed!'

'But she wouldn't've gone down like I did. Anyway, how was the rest of it? Get any tips?'

'Nothing startling. Hopkins Grocers.'

'Wouldn't touch 'em. Too much dust in their tea.'

'Harbottle Shipbuilders.'

'What mug gave you that? Didn't he know old Enoch's at death's door? Won't be worth a tin of fish without him. We'll stick to good old Bella Second, thanks. Something comfortable about gold.'

'All our eggs are in the one basket, though. There's nothing left in the bank to speak of.'

'Think of all them shares, though. Up another ten bob next week, you'll see.'

Tom shrugged. 'It's difficult not to start worrying when things are all going right.'

'Rich people do worry, love. I've noticed that. Anyway, I'm going to give a slap-up ladies' lunch. Fair's fair! I'll have a whole salmon, and so many bottles of hock that all their secrets will come tumbling out.'

'What sort of secrets?'

'Those tips you got were third-rate. Anything really good, those people keep to themselves, only their wives get to overhear 'em. I'll get it out of them.'

'Then switch some out of Bella Second?'

'You got the idea. Just as soon as my nose itches.'

The ladies' luncheon was a social success. Sarah managed to refrain from sitting down to the piano again, or teasing Mrs Sankey into blushing with double-edged remarks. It was all very decorous, and rather a let-down. Sarah emerged from it with no worthwhile inside tips. She had misjudged the occasion. What had been all right between just lady Hillingdon, Mrs Sankey and herself on that one euphoric occasion could not apply with upward of a dozen ladies present and superficial gossip holding sway. In any case, the price of Bella Second shares continued to rise. In the absence of any first-class alternatives, there was no point in selling. Nothing to do at all, except pursue an idle daily existence while waiting for the moment to sell.

'Went down to the house agent's this morning,' Thomas reported one evening. 'Thought I'd ask if there was any news about Willerby coming home and wanting it back.'

'And is he?'

'It happened they'd just heard from him. He's decided to sell. They were just going to write and ask if we'd be interested. The price is right.'

'Then why don't we take it? Whatever it is, we can afford it if we cash in the shares. They haven't moved for a week, anyway.'

'Your nose hasn't itched yet.'

'Never mind that. Let's have a drink and celebrate. Ring for old Toffee-nose. Oh, it's his evenin' off. Ring for John, then.'

The young footman came and served drinks. Sarah, who had been feeling flat all day was beginning to sparkle again. Her restless nature called for constant stimulus.

'You really think we'll take it, then?' she asked, when they had drunk a toast to success.

'Why not? If you're still set on not going to America, that is.'

'What's the point now? We don't need no land of opportunity, Tom. We found that. Anyway, I wouldn't fancy society over there.'

'You're becoming a snob.'

'I am not! We've made our circle, and we're comfortable.'

'Till old Tanby ferrets out that there never was a Watkins Motor Car Company.'

'That won't matter. Give 'em a wink and let 'em know you was bluffing all along. They admire a man who can make a pile through a bluff. Anyway, I bin thinking. I'll be glad to sell the shares now. To us, they're just bits of paper in the bank. But have you never thought of poor black men out there in Africa, workin' down in the mine? They probably get paid less than any of that lot downstairs, for all the danger and that.'

'I suppose you're right. I hadn't looked at it like that.'

'Probably hate the guts of people like us who make fortunes out of 'em without getting a finger dirty.'

'I doubt if they give it a thought. It's their living. Anyway, we take the risk with our money.'

'Fat sort of risk! Speaking of them downstairs, by the way, it's never going to work, is it? I mean, trying to make 'em appreciate friendly employers.'

'Not while old Wilson's there to keep reminding them of their places.'

'And us. I wanted to take Ethel to the Bioscope with me for company. Nearly sent him into fits. Fair tore into me.'

'I wouldn't mind swapping him; only we'd never get another as good, and the next one'd be just as nose-in-the-air. Anyway, the rest of 'em don't want to change their ways. They feel safe and cosy as they are.'

'I suppose you're right,' Sarah accepted. 'It's their lives. We'll just have to settle for bein' Lord and Lady Muck. There's worse fates . . .'

She broke off and cocked her head to one side. 'Listen. What's that music?'

Tom heard it plainly. It was tinny ragtime, obviously played on a gramophone. It came from downstairs, and ceased as abruptly as they had heard it begin.

'I know,' Tom grinned. 'They're stepping it out down there while old Misery's out of the house. Somebody was going through the pass door just then, that's why we heard it.'

'Ten to one they've got next door's cook and maid in. They're pretty thick with 'em.'

'And some beer.' He licked his lips. 'I could still fancy a brown ale.'

Sarah jumped up. 'What're we waitin' for, then? Come on!'

The din in the kitchen was so loud, and the younger servants so preoccupied with jigging about, whilst their elders and betters looked on contentedly, tumblers of ale in hand, that no one heard Thomas and Sarah slip through the pass door. They had nearly reached the foot of the stairs before they were spotted by Mrs Ambrose, who gave a little cry. John, following her startled gaze, went quickly to the gramophone and lifted the arm. Those seated began shuffling to their feet.

'Don't mind us,' Sarah told them. 'We haven't got that record. Why don't you put the other side on?'

'That ale looks good,' said Thomas. 'Don't suppose we could . . . ?'

'Get two glasses, Ethel,' ordered Mrs Ambrose, whose face was flushed. 'I'm sorry, Mrs Watkins, we was just . . .'

Sarah forestalled her, turning to the two women who did not belong in her household. 'You're Mrs Fitzgerald, aren't you?'

'Yes, madam. Cook next door. And this is Dot – Dorothy. Parlourmaid . . .'

'I hope our lot's making you welcome?'

Mrs Ambrose hastened to explain: 'We was in their place last week, madam. We take it turn and turn about.'

'Don't blame you. It's cosier down here than it is upstairs.'

'Oh, no, madam!'

'Oh, yes, Mrs Ambrose. Though I don't suppose it'd be the same if Mr Wilson was here.'

'Come on,' Thomas said. 'We don't want to spoil your fun. Let's make a party of it.'

'Yeh,' Sarah cried, accepting a tumbler of frothy brown ale. 'Where's that other side of the record?'

But while John was rewinding the gramophone before turning the disc over a chilly voice sounded from the shadowed stairway.

'In all my experience I have never encountered such an improper spectacle.'

They all turned, to see Mr Wilson descending.

'There's nothing improper about it, Wilson,' replied Thomas stoutly. 'We're just . . .'

'No, sir? It is hard to believe my eyes. I step out for an hour or two, and return to witness the order of society being overturned.' He stepped down into the kitchen. His face was white and one cheek twitching. 'The only possible explanation can be sheer ignorance. Ignorance of the behaviour proper to gentlfolk. Ignorance of the eternal and proper barrier between the classes . . .'

'Now you shut up, Wilson,' Thomas warned him. 'You're entitled to your opinion, only . . .'

'And you, *sir*,' the butler cut across him, 'may accept my notice, with immediate effect. I find this household, this whole bizarre establishment, quite intolerable. After all my years with Lord Pinner . . .'

'Sod Lord Pinner!' Sarah raged. 'You're not givin' us notice, Wilson. You're sacked, Hear it? Sacked. Fired. Order of the bleedin' boot. Got it?'

She glared from him round the stunned faces of the others. Silence lay on the air. Wilson turned abruptly and went into his pantry, shutting the door firmly. The servants shuffled their feet and looked at one another. Without a word, Thomas and Sarah left them.

'Look, Tom,' she said when they were upstairs again. 'P'raps you were right about America' There won't be no butlers bossin' us about there. This place – maybe we bit off more than we know how to chew.'

'I dunno.'

'Well, I'm beginnin' to. We sell out of Bella Second, right? Tell the agent that the chap who owns this place is welcome to it. And book First Class on the *Ocean Queen*, to a new life where money really does talk.'

'You really mean it?'

'Really. I'm fed up with this.'

'All right, then. Only, it's weekend, the Exchange won't be open till Monday.'

'In that case, let's have a little holiday. Out of this place.'

'All right. Brighton Metropole do?'

'Can't be bothered going all that way. Tell you what, Tom – the Ritz. Let's make a bloody weekend of it.'

'Done! And I'll insist on brown ale if they have to send out for it in a jug!'

He got his brown ale without demur. They ate and drank in their room, with never a qualm for the status of the people who attended them. They stayed on for a bibulous Sunday luncheon – lobster and champagne – and returned to Hyde

Park Square in a dreamlike state of mind. Ethel opened the door to them, and stammered out the news that Mr Wilson had gone, and John with him. She and Mrs Ambrose and the kitchen girl would like to stay, though.

'Never mind,' Thomas told her airily, with a wave of his arm. 'Never mind. Lot of changes, anyway. Probably going to America. Speak to Sir Joseph Weidler.'

'Yes, sir. He's here already.'

'Eh?'

'Sir Joseph Weidler, sir. Waiting in the drawing-room.'

'Oh? Well . . . Top hole, then. Just the very man!'

When they found him there, sipping a glass of whisky at this inapprorpiate hour of day, his face was grave enough to wipe the tipsy smiles off theirs. He suggested they each have one of their own drinks.

'No thanks,' said Sarah. 'Just had din . . . lunch. What's the matter, Sir Joe?'

'Appalling news. From an agent of mine in Paris, who got it from Brazaville via Tunis and heaven knows where else. The mine – Bella Second. It's caved in.'

Sarah reeled into a chair. 'Oh, no! It was so deep. I mean, the men . . . Those poor men!'

The broker said grimly. 'I'm afraid there is more to think about than the victims – it isn't known how many yet. The unfortunate truth is that the other workers have rioted and set fire to everything. They claim the mine was unsafe; that in order to bring it into production with the minimum of attention a great number of precautions were left untaken. So, what with the natural disaster and the damage caused in the riot, it seems certain to take years to open it again, if ever.'

Thomas muttered, aghast, 'Every penny we have is in it.'

Sarah moaned distractedly, 'Those poor black men! They'll all have had wives and children, and mums and dads. And this to happen, all for some rotten gold to make jewellery for the necks of daft rich women like me!'

'Is there . . . anything you can do tomorrow?' Tom asked Sir Joseph.

'They're bound to open worth a little still. A few pence each. I'll sell immediately, of course. It's fortunate that . . .' Whatever he had been on the point of saying was left unsaid. Tom sensed what it would have been: 'It's fortunate that you still have your motor car business.' But Sir Joseph had stopped himself saying it. Tom had little doubt that he knew.

Sir Joseph Weidler hurried away to carry his news to others. Thomas went to stand by one of the tall windows, looking across the Square towards other houses where it was probably already wrecking this Sunday afternoon. No one's shock and catastrophe would be likely to be as great as theirs, though. They had been in it up to the hilt. He doubted whether, by the time they had paid off the remaining servants, there would be enough left for the gas bill.

'Settles it, doesn't it?' he heard Sarah say huskily.

'Just about.'

'I mean, we aren't committed to the house?'

'No, no.'

'Not enough left to get to America?'

'Need more than that.'

'Well – it was all right, for a bit.'

'Comfortable, while it lasted.'

'I didn't fancy it much. Servants, and things.'

'Seen how the other half live.'

He heard her get up and come to him. Her arm went into his and they looked out over the Square together.

'We still got each other,' said Sarah.

'Yeh,' Thomas said.

CHAPTER THIRTEEN

They did have enough for the gas bill, and for the rest of the outstanding bills besides. Fortunately, the shares they held had all been paid for. What little there was over after paying off Wilson, Mrs Ambrose and the others enabled them to move into lodgings for a week or so; enough time to collect their wits and find something else. They had slipped away from Hyde Park Square without leaving a trace of themselves. Thomas Watkins, motor manufacturer, and his wife Sarah had gone from the face of the earth. Thomas Watkins, opportunist, and Sarah Moffat, sank back into the quicksand of London, from which they had briefly struggled free.

They didn't drown, though. They went to Grimshaw's employment agency to tell a characteristic tale of multiple qualifications and unsullied background. Mr Grimshaw, a cynic, offered them domestic service. They accepted.

So it was that they found themselves, one clammy evening at dusk, alighting from a branch-line train in the quiet of rural Wiltshire. Rain was falling. In the flickering gaslight there stood no one to meet them. They went outside and stood under the wooden canopy, looking round. Sarah shivered.

'Just like arriving in your bloomin' Wales. Only there was supposed to be a reception comittee this time. Where is it?'

'They said he'd send a car to pick us up.'

'Well?'

'I don't know, do I? It'll be along.'

Half an hour later it was Thomas who was doing the complaining. They had set off to trudge through dark lanes, peering at names on the gates of sparsely-scattered houses. 'There'll be a car to meet us, indeed! I knew it would turn out like this. I know a rat when I smell one.'

'We was lucky to get the job, so shut up moaning. You've done nothin' else.'

'Now who's talking? Anyway, going back into service isn't a job. It's slavery.'

'Here it is,' Sarah said, though with little relief in her tone. They had come to a gateway wider than most of the others, with pointed white posts and a long gate, on the top bar of which she had made out the name THE MANOR. It was an unwelcoming sort of gate, sagging on its hinges, its paintwork flaked away, overhung by dripping laurel leaves. Thomas had to heave it up bodily to get the latch unfastened. The surface of the drive under their feet was sticky and broken. Dark shrubs lowered on each side.

The house they soon came to proved no more inviting. From what they could see of it in the near-darkness it had been a fine old place, but now it was shabby, shuttered, neglected. There was no glimmer of light at all.

They trudged to up to the front door. It looked as implacable as if it had not been opened for years. Sarah jerked at a bell-pull, but they heard no sound. She dragged at it again, and it came away in her hand. Thomas took it and tried to replace it. While he was doing so she gave the door an experimental push. It creaked open. There was still no light.

'Hello!' called Thomas, peering into the blackness. 'Hello!'

There came no responding sound. Sarah said helpfully, 'There doesn't seem to be anyone here.'

'You know, I was getting that very same impression. Maybe we've come to the wrong house.'

'Can't be. It said The Manor, so it must be the bloomin' Manor. More likely we got the wrong day.'

' 'Course we haven't. Old Grimshaw said tomorrow, didn't he? Well, tomorrow's today. I have a distinct feeling we've been well and truly had.'

'Yeh. After paying the old bugger a week's wages in advance. We'll just have to go back to London.'

'We can't. That porter was locking the station. Anyway,

we spent the last of our cash on the tickets. We're marooned in this place, all because of you.'

'Me? Why blame me?'

'You were the one who didn't mind going back into service. "Gentleman's residence" indeed! "Nestling in the folds of the Wiltshire Downs." We've been had.'

'Listen!' Sarah silenced him with a hiss. The distant sound of a piano, slow and wistful, reached their ears.

They entered the house fully, closing the front door quietly. Tom groped for a light-switch, but couldn't find one. Now that they were growing used to the interior gloom, though, a faint streak of light under a doorway became discernible. They crept towards it, hand in hand, picking up their feet in instinctive fear of broken boards. The piano was growing louder, not only because they were getting nearer to it, but because the music had suddenly changed from sublime to passionate. Tom knocked at the door of the room, but it was obvious that he could not be heard. He pushed open the door and they stood there, looking in.

Two candles gave all the illumination there was. The furniture was cloaked in white dust-sheets. In the centre of the pool of light stood the piano, with the candlesticks on it. It, too, was sheeted, but the sheet had been rolled back. The player was a man. Sarah thought he looked about Thomas's age and build, and not altogether unlike him, only his hair was wild and gold-rimmed spectacles glinted over his eyes. He seemed to be staring at the keyboard as he played. A bottle of brandy stood on the piano top in front of him.

They stood there silent until he stopped playing with a flourish, throwing up both hands. Then he grabbed the bottle and raised it to his lips. The action of tilting his head to drink brought his eyes up to see them, but he didn't interrupt his prolonged swig. After it he wiped his mouth with the back of a hand and asked, 'Who're you?'

'Sorry,' Sarah said, advancing. 'We did knock. We're the new staff.'

'Staff?'

'Watkins, sir,' said Thomas. 'Thomas and Sarah Watkins, sent by Grimshaw and Linnet. You'll be Mr de Brassey, I take it?'

'We're a bit late,' Sarah explained, when no answer came, ' 'cos there was no one at the station to meet us, and Mr Grimshaw said there would be.'

The man spoke again at last. His voice was not slurred, but had the dry precision of the constant drinker who has come to terms with his condition.

'I wrote to Grimshaw two weeks ago, cancelling the request. That's why I'm not expecting you. Not expecting anybody.'

'But you got to be!' Sarah cried.

Tom said, 'I think there must be some misunderstanding, sir. Whatever instructions you sent to Mr Grimshaw can never have reached him. Otherwise he would never have sent us all the way here, at considerable expense to ourselves.'

'I have his acknowledgement,' was the bleak reply. 'By letter.'

Sarah stepped closer to the candlelight, which fell full on her face now. The pianist stared at her. She asked plaintively, 'What the hell are we meant to do now, then?'

He seemed to rouse himself a little. 'If it's a question of money . . .'

'No, thank you,' Thomas said, though Sarah gave him a sharp dig with her elbow for it. 'We're not asking for charity.'

'Don't be such a damn' fool,' the man retorted. 'Of course you'll be recompensed. Only you can't go anywhere tonight. You can stay here. You'll find the kitchen and the servants' quarters.'

He picked up the bottle and drank again. Then he bent to the keyboard and resumed his playing, again on a wistful note. They watched him for some minutes, but he didn't look up. Thomas nudged Sarah and they crept from the room unseen.

There was electric light in the large kitchen, but what it

revealed was anything but agreeable. The central table was piled high with pots, pans, bottles and jars, all of which proved to be soiled or to hold mildewed contents. Unwashed dishes filled the sink. Utensils, crockery, food containers and cloths were strewn everywhere. Empty brandy and wine bottles were prominent amongst the chaos.

Tom went through to the servant's quarters and soon came back.

'I'm not sleeping in there,' he said. 'Not fit for a pig.'

'I couldn't sleep in this place, anyway,' Sarah said. Rain and wind were rattling the windows and the house itself seemed to be shaking. 'Let's clear a couple of chairs and get a bit of rest. P'raps he'll have sobered up in the morning.'

But she had been right when she said she would not be able to sleep. Some time after midnight she got up from her cramped position and put on the light. Thomas, who, she'd always said, could sleep on a clothes-line if he had to, never even blinked. Sarah found a tolerable apron and put it on. She rolled up her sleeves and started to tackle the mess.

She was still at it well after dawn when the door from the yard opened and a man came in. She recognised the piano player, now wearing a heavy overcoat and a broad-brimmed hat. He stared at her, then at Tom, mouth open in a chair. His eyes travelled round the cleaned-up kitchen.

'I couldn't sleep,' she said.

'You shouldn't have done this, though. Mrs Dobson comes in from the village.'

'Once in a blue moon, from the look of it. What's the rest of the house like?'

'Just as bad. Look, I'm sorry about last night. I must have seemed rude.'

'Bloomin' rude.'

'I was . . . drunk. I didn't expect anyone. I told you, I'd cancelled my request for staff. The place is going to be sold.'

'Oh yeh? Like to know who'd buy it in this state. I'd say you need staff more 'n ever, if you really want to get a price.

We'd do it for you, if Thomas agrees. Wouldn't take that long. 'Course, we'd expect to be paid.'

'I'll think about it.'

'Yeh. Only if Thomas agrees, though.'

Having almost no alternative, Thomas did agree. So did Mr Richard de Brassey. At least, he didn't disagree, but seemed to consent with his silence. He had gone to his bedroom and shut himself in. With what edible supplies she could find Sarah cooked a meal for them all. Thomas took a tray upstairs, but there was no response to his knocking at the door.

'Boozing again, I expect,' he said when he came down and prepared to eat the food himself. 'Not worth bothering with him.'

'Full of the milk of human kindness, Thomas Watkins, aren't you? That poor man needs looking after.'

'He can look after himself. I don't know why you let us into this.'

'We might as well do it. It'll be a roof over our heads for a few days while you think up some new bright idea. He'll be bound to pay us something for it. I mean, there'll be no harm done.'

'Yes,' Thomas said, 'but why bother cleaning the place up?'

'You said it's not fit for a pig, and I'm not even a pig. Besides, what else is there to do? We've got to face up to it, Tom – we've got nothing bleedin' else now.'

He capitulated. Between them they got the kitchen completely to rights. Then they ventured further afield. They found a dining-room and a nice, classical drawing-room, completely neglected. They set about the drawing-room, and Thomas found himself warming to the work. Mr de Brassey appeared late in the day, drunk but controlled, and said he would give them three pounds a week for as long as the cleaning-up process needed. Sarah mentioned food. He said she could get Mrs Dobson to bring in enough for them, but that he wasn't interested. Yet she managed to talk him into taking some broth and bread and butter, before disappearing again. That evening they heard his piano playing. they thought they had better not intrude.

A good night in a cleaned-up bedroom restored them both. They were startled while eating breakfast, though, to hear the clatter of a horse's hooves. Thomas rose to his feet and craned his neck to see out of the window.

'It's him!' he exclaimed. 'Going off riding, in his state.'

'How do you know what state he's in?'

'I can guess.'

'Better not go very fast, then.'

But he did 'go fast'. When Tom went out later to fetch some logs from a pile near the end of the driveway, where a field adjoined, he was astonished to see the same black horse he had seen from the window leaping hedges. It was coming nearer, galloping towards another hedge intervening. Again it sailed over, rushing on towards a low stone wall. Thomas watched in fascinated alarm as the rider skilfully lined up his mount for the approach.

It surged forward, but at that moment there was an explosion, probably from the gun of a farmhand in a thicket not far off, potting at a rabbit, loud and startling enough to make the horse falter, shy, and refuse. Its rider came over its neck and crashed down head first against the wall. The horse shook itself and cantered away, as Thomas dropped the firewood and ran for all he was worth.

He bent over the crumpled form. The big hat had fallen off, and blood was oozing freely from Richard de Brassey's temple: he was quite unconscious. Without thinking to consider other possible injuries, Thomas picked him up and carried him bodily to the house.

'I've warned him more than once about his riding,' said the peppery old doctor, as he packed his bag. 'Told him the next fall could be the last fall. He doesn't seem to care. Don't suppose he's been eating?' Sarah shook her head.

'And as for his drinking – well. We must just hope it's only concussion, and he doesn't slide into a coma. I'm afraid if that should happen, in de Brassey's physical state

. . .' The doctor shook his head and prepared to leave.

'I should have thought he ought to be in hospital,' Thomas said.

'As it happens,' replied the doctor coldly, 'the nearest hospital is over sixty miles away, and most probably he wouldn't survive the journey. I'll look in tomorrow morning. Good day.'

Somebody would have to be constantly beside the injured man, the doctor had said. Very well, they agreed, they would take turns to watch. They sat with him through the night, first Thomas, then Sarah, their eyes on the pale, still face, in the dim bedroom, softly lit by an oil-lamp, its wick turned down. Thomas shook his head as Sarah took over as the stable-clock chimed four.

'Seems to be sinking, if anything,' Thomas said.

'Oh, God.' She sat down on the other side of the bed. Suddenly she looked up. 'You know, perhaps there's something we can do. I read in this magazine or something that some people believe you can actually *will* sick people better. Something to do with the electricity in our bodies. Well? Worth a go, i'n't it? Nothing to lose by trying. I got Powers, you know.'

Thomas shrugged, but followed Sarah's example in taking one of Richard's hands. She smiled at him, closed her eyes, and began to 'will'.

Darkness gave way to dawn-light. Thomas was asleep, the limp hand still in his, but she hung grimly on to her consciousness, her lips moving steadily in a prayer, until suddenly, irresistibly, weariness overcame her and she slept.

A cock crowed in a nearby farm-yard. Through the window came the first rays of the sun, touching Richard's face with gold. His eyes opened, to see the two of them, their hands both holding his. Gently he tried to withdraw them, but the slight movement was enough.

Awake, they smiled at him, then at each other. The spell had worked.

Sarah seemed to have performed more magic than she

intended. Not only did Richard's condition improve rapidly, much to the cynical doctor's surprise, but the sick despair which had lain on him when they had first come to the Manor had lifted. He was more normal, more cheerful; and the night of vigil had in some remarkable way brought the three of them very close together. Soon he was well enough to be helped downstairs to the drawing-room, now transformed by Sarah. Clean, bright, swept and polished, its fire-irons reflected a great log-fire, and spring flowers gathered by Sarah from the neglected gardens filled every vase she could find. Here, in perfect amity, Thomas and Richard wrangled placidly over a chessboard, and Thomas instructed him in various little skills he had picked up in his travels, such as the three-card trick, Find the Lady, assisted by Sarah, nearly as skilled herself. The stakes for which they played were unusual: sandwiches, tea-cakes, sponge fingers and macaroons. And Richard, who invariably lost, was by decree obliged to eat them. He ate quite well these days – Sarah saw to that – and instead of wine on the table, there was tea.

That is, until the night of Richard's birthday. For that there was to be a special celebration, with champagne. Richard wore a modified version of evening dress, with a picturesque ruffled shirt, every inch the squire of the Manor, and Thomas and Sarah, with no wardrobes to call on; had raided the attic. It was one of those attics children dream of, containing trunks full of old 'dressing-up' clothes. The dead-and-gone de Brasseys had taken good care of their garments, it seemed. Sarah had found an enchanting dress from somewhere about the turn of the eighteenth century, all muslin, ribbons and lace, which transformed her into the likeness of a porcelain Bow figure. Thomas's disguise was perhaps not quite so much in period, the effect of his silken coat and breeches and embroidered waistcoat being a little offset by his twentieth-century moustache. But Sarah thought he looked grand enough to curtsey to, before turning to be admired by Richard.

'You look quite beautiful,' Richard said.

'I thought I looked rather lovely, too,' said Thomas wistfully.

'Oo, we found some smashing things up there,' Sarah told Richard. 'All sorts – and the most beautiful old-fashioned wedding-dress.'

He smiled. 'I remember that. It was my grandmother's.' He opened the champagne and poured.

Sarah raised her glass. 'Happy birthday.' Thomas echoed her, and the three friends drank.

Later, Richard played the piano; Chopin, he told them, a waltz; and Thomas and Sarah tried to dance to it, and found that Chopin waltzes are not for dancing. Richard came to their rescue with a gramophone, which also enabled him to take his turn with Sarah, while Thomas happily looked on and automatically raised his champagne-glass to his lips. He must have done this too automatically, for by about eleven o'clock he was feeling that he would be happier lying down. Rather than admit to his condition he told them with mustered dignity that he was tired and was going to bed, but not to mind him, and go on enjoying themselves.

They played no more music after he had gone, but went to sit on either side of the fire.

'I seem to have come to know you so well,' Richard said, 'and yet I don't know you at all – either of you. Will you tell me how you come to be here at all?'

Sarah did so, retracing the whole sequence of events of rags to riches to rags again. In doing so, she realised how remarkably it all linked together, one thing leading to another almost as if someone, somewhere, was forging each new link in readiness to add it on. It was a long chain already, but he listened without interrupting.

'Coo!' she said at length. 'Look at the time!'

'Never mind the time, Sarah. Not tonight. It's a change to talk.'

'Yeh, it is. You haven't told me about you yet.'

'Oh, mine's not half as varied a story as yours.'

'I'd like to hear it, though. Tell you what, will I make us some cocoa? Don't want any more booze, do we?'

He accepted willingly. when she came back he asked something which he had evidently been pondering while she was gone.

'How long have you been married?'

She hesitated only momentarily. 'Tell you the truth, we aren't. We just . . . go round together.'

He smiled. 'Elsie Maynard and Jack Point.'

'You what?'

'Gilbert and Sullivan. *The Yeomen of the Guard* or the Merryman and his Maid.'

'Something like that. We seem to stick, Gawd knows why sometimes. Come on, though. Tell me about you.'

She saw his expression change, become somehow guarded. He sounded artificially casual when he answered, 'Oh, pretty standard for my sort. My father died three years ago and left me this place. I never wanted to live here, but Elizabeth – my wife – she did.' He laughed suddenly, harshly. 'When she'd finished doing the place up to her taste she bolted, with the man who trained our horses. We had a lot of horses then.'

'Bad luck for you.'

He shrugged. 'It was an arranged marriage. My parents' acres became engaged to her parents' acres, and then got married. That's all there is to it.'

Sarah was looking at him shrewdly. 'Then why'd you take it so bad? Get into the state you was when we came here?'

'Oh . . . well, I was drinking, you know, and . . .'

'And what, Richard? Tell me. I've owned up to you.'

She moved suddenly, to sit on the floor next to his chair, her face towards the dying fire, instinctively sparing him the embarrassment of being looked at while he spoke. Equally instinctively, his hand came down to rest on her shoulder. He replied flatly, 'It was the fire. You've seen the damage to the first floor of the wing. It was . . . six months tomorrow. My small daughter was . . . was burned to death. She was four years old.'

For a moment Sarah said nothing. Then, still not looking at him, 'I don't know what that's like – to lose your child.'

'No.'

'But I do know what it's like to lose babies. I've had three die. Well . . . They weren't all . . . even so. I mean, they died.'

Richard moved from his chair to sit beside her on the floor. They gazed into the flames, each seeing different pictures there.

'The worst thing is the guilt,' he said.

'I know a bit about that, too.'

'You always feel you could have . . .' He could hardly go on. 'If only . . . You can't help it.'

'If, if!' she said gently. 'With an *if* you can put the moon in a bottle.'

She was saying the right things to him, taking it the right way.

'I've never talked about it to anyone. But I knew you'd understand.'

Sarah put her hand to his cheek in a tender gesture. He turned it towards his lips, kissing the palm. It was as far as he would have gone; but Sarah drew his face towards hers, and for the first time they kissed. The thing that had been between them was at last acknowledged.

As Richard lay in bed that night remorse set in. He should never have kissed Sarah, never have let her see what she had awakened in him, which was no less than love. For there was Thomas: and for Thomas, too, he felt a kind of love, the response to all Thomas's friendship and kindness to him, when he needed it so sorely. The feeling which linked the unlikely triangle took no account of class difference or their short acquaintanceship. He could not wound it by hurting Thomas, however badly he wanted Sarah.

As so he went back into his shell, not drinking as much as he once had done but remaining in his room, refusing all food. It was Thomas who finally got through that resolutely-closed door with a breakfast tray.

Richard was sitting by the fireplace, huddled in his dressing-gown.

'I don't want any breakfast,' he said without looking up.

'It's only tea and toast. Sarah says you've got to eat it.'

'That all you wanted to say to me?' was the moody response.

Thomas put down the tray and advanced. 'No. What I wanted to say was what the bloody hell's the matter with you?' Disregarding Richard's startled, angry reaction, he went on. 'We haven't seen you for two days.'

'You don't have to worry about me,' Richard snapped. 'I am perfectly all right – thank you.'

'You don't look it.'

'How I look is my own damn affair!'

Thomas critically surveyed the scatter of empty wine-bottles on the floor. 'Your funeral,' he said, beginning to pick them up.

The other's temper flashed out. 'Just watch what you say, damn you! You'd do very well to remember . . .'

'. . . my place?' Thomas finished for him, sarcastically. 'Yes, sir, Mr de Brassey, sir.'

Richard knew he had let himself betray their friendship and hated himself for it, as he had hated himself when he kissed Sarah. 'Go to hell,' he muttered.

'Anything you say, sir,' Thomas mocked. 'Will that be all, sir?'

Richard buried his face in his hands. 'Oh, for Christ's sake, Thomas!'

'Look . . . If you'd prefer that I went –'

Richard reached out and clutched his arm. 'I don't want you to go, Thomas.'

Thomas knew that something important was about to be said. 'You don't want me to go, or you don't want Sarah to go?'

'I don't want either of you to go. You must understand that. I can't explain . . . I . . .'

Thomas was regarding him evenly, dispassionately. 'If you're worried about Sarah and me – or if I may put it even more indelicately, if you're worried about Sarah and you – you don't have to. There hasn't been anything between Sarah and me for – for a very long time now.'

Richard looked up, surprised. 'Sarah said . . .'

Thomas smiled. ' "Sarah said." Sarah, my friend, has a propensity for highly romantic flights of fancy.'

He saw that Richard had taken the point by the relaxation of the tense face. Relief, the banishment of guilt.

'Good,' said Thomas with satisfaction. 'Now will you eat your bloody breakfast?'

That evening he was downstairs again, shaved, sober, restored to near-normal, and playing his favourite Chopin, Sarah listening. Richard looked round as he finished the piece.

'Thomas not in?'

'He's putting the pony in.'

'Damn!'

'Why damn? He likes that little pony.'

'Damn because I shouldn't have forgotten. I've never forgotten before.'

She understood the note in his voice. 'Oh, it was your little girl's, was it? Well, there's no harm done, Tom's perfectly capable. You're really only punishing yourself quite unnecessarily, you know. Come on, play me something.'

'What would you like. Some Chopin?'

'That all you can play?' she teased.

'It's all I want to play. "Cannons hidden in flowers." Someone once said that about Chopin – about his nationalism. It was Schubert, actually. "Cannons hidden in flowers." '

'Not like you. You're all cannons hiding the flowers.'

His hands left the keys. 'Sarah. I have something to say to you.'

She came to his side. 'No, you don't. You and I don't have to say anything to each other.' She put a kiss on the tip of her finger and laid it on his mouth. Their eyes met in a long, understanding look.

Next morning Thomas woke from a heavy sleep, the result of his labours to restore the gardens to something like their previous condition. He turned over towards Sarah's side of the bed, to find it empty, un-slept in.

In the kitchen, as he entered, Richard and Sarah were having breakfast. Both, he noticed with mild surprise, were wearing the clothes they had worn the evening before.

'Ah, good morning,' he said. 'All up nice and early.'

'We haven't been to bed,' Sarah told him. Richard looked down at his coffee-cup, saying nothing.

'Oh yes? So what kept you two up all night, then?'

'We were talking.'

'Really? So you were talking all night, were you? Must have had a lot to say to each other.'

'Yes, we did,' said Sarah. She glanced across the table at Richard, who shook his head slightly, but she went on. 'Thomas, Richard wants me to marry him.'

Thomas lightly touched the coffee-pot, glanced at his finger as though it were burnt, and went to the tap, where he ran water over it. All this gave time for him to take in and react to what he had just been told. When he spoke, it was to say, quite calmly, 'That's marvellous.'

'Yes, yes, it is, isn't it?' Sarah cried, while Richard watched him anxiously, finally getting up from the table.

'Thomas,' he said. 'I'm sorry – it's a bit sudden . . .'

'Sudden? If two people decide to get married, what's sudden got to do with it? Now – who wants more coffee?'

Richard was acutely embarrassed. 'I've one or two things to do, and I'm sure you want to talk to Sarah. So I'll go.'

Thomas waved him down. 'No, no. On the contrary. You stay right where you are. If anyone's going to do any going, that person's going to be me. You're the two who will want to be alone, and then when you get married you'll hardly want me hanging round the shop, will you, playing the old gooseberry.'

'But of course we will,' Richard said. 'We shall want you with us always. You're our friend. It's still just the three of us. So you mustn't go.'

' 'Course he mustn't,' echoed Sarah.

Thomas looked from one to the other. 'No?'

'Of course not,' she repeated.

He sat down again. There was so much he wanted to say to Sarah, knowing her as he did. He wanted to ask her if she knew what she was doing, not only for her sake, but for Richard's, because Richard was his friend; perhaps the only friend he had ever had. But the words would not come to him. Perhaps it was better to leave it as it was.

Sarah had brought down the old wedding-dress from the attic and was altering it to fit herself. It was fragile, elaborate, and enchanting. Richard watched her as she put the finishing touches to it.

'Don't let's ask anybody to the wedding,' he said. 'Let there be just you, and me, and Thomas, as best man. There's a little chapel on the estate – you can't see it from here, but I can show you the general direction.' He took her to the window. 'See those trees behind the small barn –' As they looked, his grip on her arm tightened sharply. 'My God, what's going on? There's smoke coming from the barn! Oh my God, quickly!'

He rushed out of the room, Sarah following him. The old wedding-dress slipped to the floor, a needle still in its hem.

The small barn with the hay-loft above it blazed fiercely in the evening breeze. In the yard farm-hands fought it vainly, flinging bucket after bucket of water on to the flames. When Richard appeared among them the noise was such that he had to shout.

'What the bloody hell happened?'

'Dunno, Mr Richard, sir,' replied one, who was tending to a man overcome by smoke. 'One of the men must bin smokin'.'

'Dear God, I've told you all about that! Someone gone for the Brigade?'

'Yes, sir, young Harry.'

Sarah was looking round anxiously. 'Where's Thomas?'

Richard shook the man's shoulder. 'Williams! Where's Thomas?'

'Ain't he come out, sir? He went in to get Miss Madeleine's pony.'

'To get the pony!' Richard tore off his jacket. 'The bloody fool, he'll be killed!' He rushed off towards the barn, Sarah after him.

'Richard, Richard, what are you going to do?'

'Get Thomas out of there!' he shouted over his shoulder. Just at that moment the barn door gave way and collapsed, giving out a burst of flame and showing an inferno within the barn. The terrified pony rushed out, eyes staring, and bolted away but Richard was trying to see through the flames, edging nearer and shouting for Thomas. Sarah caught at him.

'You can't go in there, Richard! You'll be killed. Richard!'

But he had flung his arm across his mouth and was gone through the billowing smoke, into the red hell of the barn. A fearful crash told them that a supporting timber had come down, sending flames up through the roof and driving the spectators further back across the yard. Sarah shrieked and prayed. Then out of the smoke someone staggered, only just discernible, another figure across his shoulder, both blackened and unrecognisable. Sarah ran towards them, screaming their names.

In the little graveyard of the chapel the priest was ending the Burial Service, watched by a small crowd of mourers. In the field below, the rescued pony grazed obliviously.

'In sure and certain hope of the Resurrection to Eternal Life,' intoned the priest. Sarah stepped forward and dropped a rose on the coffin, now lowered by the bearers to the bottom of the grave.

The service was over, the scattering of mourners beginning to drift away, murmuring. Sarah, blank-eyed, took the arm of the man standing protectively beside her. For a time they had been Thomas and Sarah and Richard; now they were just Thomas and Sarah again.

And don't miss the first book based on London Weekend's immensely popular television series starring PAULINE COLLINS and JOHN ALDERTON

THOMAS AND SARAH

Mollie Hardwick

DOWNSTAIRS ON ITS UPPERS . . .

When Thomas, the Welsh chauffeur, and Sarah, the nursery maid, leave the security of Eaton Place, they find that the world owes no one – not even them – a living.

THOMAS AND SARAH continues the story of the two popular characters from UPSTAIRS, DOWNSTAIRS to tell how they get by – with wit, cunning and infinite ability to make a few pence where they can. Of course, they have one or two advantages. At the beginning, for instance, unofficial access to Mr Bellamy's Rolls-Royce . . .

FICTION/TV TIE-IN 0 7221 0512 6 85p